Hell & Other Novels

M.Reed

Other Works by Beverley Daurio

INTERNAL DOCUMENT *(Streetcar Editions, 1992)*
HIS DOGS *(Underwhich Editions, 1990)*
JUSTICE *(Moonstone Press, 1988)*
IF SUMMER HAD A KNIFE *(Wolsak & Wynn, 1987)*
NEXT IN LINE *(Identity, 1982)*

HELL & other NOVELS

Beverley DAURIO

COACH HOUSE PRESS • TORONTO

© Beverley Daurio, 1992

Published with the assistance of the Canada Council,
the Department of Communications, the Ontario Arts Council
and the Ontario Ministry of Culture and Communications.

Lyrics from the song 'Sudbury Saturday Night' by Tom Connors
© Crown-Vetch Music (a division of Stompin' Tom Ltd.).
Used by permission.

Canadian Cataloguing in Publication Data
Daurio, Beverley, 1953-
    Hell & other novels
ISBN 0-88910-421-2
I. Title.
PS8557.A87H44 1992   C813'.54   C92-095103-1
PR9199.3.D387H44 1992

For Don

Contents

EQUINOX / 11
MANY MOTHERS / 27
THREE MONTHS / 49
BLACK BRANCH IN YELLOW WIND / 65
**THE BEAUTIFUL VOICES OF
THE MONKS BEHIND THE WALL / 77**
BIG OZ / 95
HIS DOGS / 113
EIGHT SCENES: SOME TANGLED, SOME PLAIN / 121
***HELL* & OTHER NOVELS / 135**

Acknowledgements

I am grateful to my editor, Gail Scott, and to Susan Swan; to Daniel Jones, for his time and critical notations; to Libby Scheier, for advice; and to David Lee, Steve Heighton, Jenny Lee, and Sonja Skarstedt for their comments and encouragement. Donald Daurio provided incisive readings of these texts in their early and final stages, for which I thank him.

Financial assistance from the Canada Council, the Ontario Arts Council (through the Writers' Reserve and Works in Progress Programs), and the Barbara Deming Memorial Fund (Brooklyn, New York) made it possible to complete this book.

Sections from 'Eight Scenes: Some Tangled, Some Plain' were published in *Snapshots: Short Short Fiction* (Black Moss Press, 1992). Other pieces from this book, in earlier incarnations, have previously appeared or are forthcoming in: *Quarry, This Magazine, Black Apple, Canadian Fiction Magazine, Prairie Fire, Onion, The Malahat Review, Meanjin* (Australia), and *West Coast Line*. *His Dogs* was first published as a limited edition chapbook (Underwhich Editions, 1990).

EQUINOX

◆ Early Saturday morning, a courier in a helmet and a blue and orange suit wheels her bicycle up my sidewalk and hands me a thick white envelope. It takes a minute to pry open the flap and tweeze out the papers inside because my arms and hands are shaking. My divorce is final. I go to the edge of the porch and whisper *Hallelujah!* seven or eight times. My neighbour, Paul, stops weeding his marigolds and leans on his side of the fence, watching me. I am sick with a pagan, absolute joy. I say, *Yee-hah!* and the spirit in me rages like a madwoman locked in an attic.

This morning should be serene and golden, but instead there is a wild sky boiling in the wind over the houses. Low clouds of yellow and grey drift to the northwest above the roofs, away from the lake. I have spent half my life unmarried, and half my life married. I don't know what comes next.

My oldest son, Joey, is hiding in the living room, staring at the wall. I see his point. I see why he doesn't approve of me celebrating—partly because it confirms the dark things he has so recently become obsessed with, I know that—and partly because it is his father's absence I am dancing on. But I'm tired of being the stable one, the one who holds everything together by thinking, and I manage to ignore him.

Paul and I sit outside and drink the fresh lemonade he brought over in a crystal pitcher with two glasses on a tray to help me celebrate. Behind us, my second son, David, opens and closes the curtains in disgust. Joey doesn't try to make him stop and I don't blame him. David flips the curtains with a sound like moths against the glass, and I can feel Joey with his back to me in the leather chair that used to be my husband's, the high-backed brown chair where Eric lounged and smoked and drank. I sit on the front steps that need painting and think about what colour to paint them. I talk to Paul while Joey sits, sullen and fourteen, in Eric's big chair. Joey stares at blankness and tries to make himself up out of nothing.

I am thinking that the porch steps should be teal blue, and that the street is quiet for a Saturday. The wind blows dandelion seed that sticks in my hair and in Paul's, and the noises that we hear are the quiet rational sounds of plants and animals. I wish the secrets we discover about one another could occasionally be surprising in a pleasant way: that Teddy Hicks across the street was a distress-line volunteer, for instance, instead of a hustler; or that Eric had abandoned Joey, not to a criss-crossing of thirsty shadows against a curtain, but to beauty and a clearer fate.

Beside me, Paul is saying that I need a man like Granger. Paul has a list of good things to say about him, but I'm not so sure. The first time Granger came over to my place he went right to the refrigerator and looked inside.

Wow, you've got tons of food, he said.

I have two kids, I said. *They need to eat.*

Granger works at breaking things, demolishing buildings. He runs a crusher, or aims an iron wrecking ball at the correct point in the supporting wall so that the bricks seem to explode out to meet it. With the sound of an avalanche, the bricks crash down, exposing ancient crooked beams and broken-open rooms with stripped interiors.

It's a hollow kind of day; it needs detail. I'd be equally happy taking all the crystal glasses Eric and I collected over the years, mostly as wedding and anniversary presents, and smashing them against the back fence—or drinking dusty champagne and strawberry juice toasts out of them until I passed out.

Instead, I phone Granger and we go to a québécois film after lunch. It's hot outside and cool in the theatre. The seat upholstery is bristly and stiff against the bare parts of our legs. Eight adults talk about death and sex and the collapse of their culture. The only part Granger likes is the men talking about how hard it is to find the clitoris, and how much work it is to bring a woman to orgasm. He laughs. These men prefer to pay for it, they say, because then the focus is where it belongs, on the penis. During the bodyrub parlour scene I feel Granger and the other men in the audience straining toward the woman's creamy hand, wanting it. To pay for it.

Granger used to go out Saturday nights wandering around looking for it for free. Getting it for free and keeping the focus where it belonged at the same time was the ultimate. *Men only brag about paying for it in movies,* Granger says to me, as if he is the only man I've ever met, and he's translating something that I wouldn't understand. Under my thin cotton sweater, against the small of my back, he rubs his hand up and down.

During the seven months it took my marriage to disintegrate it rained every night and I spent a lot of time in theatres. I left David with Joey and became one dark shape among many, my face turned up toward the bright screen, crying. The smell of popcorn still makes me sad, especially in the afternoon if there are wet umbrellas slipping shut. Granger doesn't say anything. He hands me a napkin.

EQUINOX

Granger and I get back to my place about five. The day is still bright, and what's left of the brief afternoon rain is drying on clean sidewalks.

Sometimes I'm lucky. Sometimes I'm not so lucky—when I get snagged on an idea and watch it pull me along, for instance. I've only been in love twice, once with my ex-husband, Eric, and once with a native guy I met up north. My friend Catherine says I am too picky, and that's one of the things I've heard a lot since I told Eric to move out.

Granger looks good standing beside my open refrigerator with a tomato in his hand. He looks good when he takes a bite out of the tomato. He is tall and has wavy light-brown hair parted in the middle. His wire-rimmed glasses appear nicely ironic above his muscles and the tan he gets operating heavy equipment outdoors. And then, over his skin, tank tops, tight jeans, that sort of thing.

You have to concentrate on what's good about a person, Catherine says. That's among the things I hear a lot that I don't understand at all.

Catherine sits on a green wooden chair across the kitchen table from me and watches red juice running from the bite in the tomato down Granger's arm. She watches him lick the juice off the inside of his wrist. When Granger isn't here, Catherine says he's mindless.

She never asks me questions about Granger; she tells me, as if she knows him better than I do. I don't argue with her.

The day is all lit up and white at the edges, smouldering. I want to get Joey settled with instructions and let the fresh air outside caress the bare skin of my arms and face. I want to hear the screen door slam behind me.

Catherine stares at Granger, wedged into the cool open refrigerator. It's as if she's dying to ask him to shut the fridge door, but can't figure out what to say. I think she wants to tell him to do something, just to see if he will. Maybe she's waiting for an emotion to form around him for her. It's hard to tell.

As soon as Joey gets home, the three of us can pile into Granger's Buick and go to the beer store. Catherine's never driven in Granger's red car, and that's one of the reasons I'm eager to go; I want to watch her reaction. He drives like a maniac, and I feel uncertain, I feel like he's going to let me down when he drives too fast. I get the sense that he's almost mishandling the car on purpose, to see if he can slide so close to his fear of death that he can physically push it away.

I think, *where is Joey?*—and I know—in one of those indivertible pictures I get of things I'd rather not see—where Eric is: telling his story to some barmaid with kohl around her eyes, eyes empty of experience and full of hope. He touches her arm near the elbow lightly, as if he doesn't dare. He makes her laugh and cry. Eric forgets. This is his biggest and most consistent skill. What really happens doesn't happen for him. The night he walked out without saying goodbye to Joey and David, the day he dumped a pot of stew on the carpet—for Eric, those times are spent and gone like the matches piling up in the ashtray on the bar in front of him.

I was sure at one time that David was conceived supernaturally—no sex with Eric for months, and I wouldn't have done anything else but touch myself, not then. Later I guessed Eric must have got to me in my sleep, maybe even in his sleep, too, because he said he didn't remember. But Joey is his father's son without a doubt, in body and in movement, and sometimes it makes him hate his hands, the sharp white bones in his cheeks. At these times Joey suspects me of confusing him with his father, and his holiness abandons him, to be replaced by any human characteristics he can bear to imagine.

Catherine and Granger are talking about where we should go tonight. Catherine phones Paul to ask him what he thinks. I don't care as long as it's loud. I look out into my godless backyard, the flattened grass under the bats and balls the kids left lying around, the picket fence, the pastel garages. Everywhere the elastic sound of things moving, the giant crayfish noise of car brakes, a radio playing Brubeck turned way up. I remember Eric's hand on a grey knife handle, and how the tender flesh of his fingers there was more frightening than the cold blade at my throat.

Pig, I say to the window, under my breath, but then I stop. Let him remember.

Seeing Granger with the nub of tomato, which is all that remains in his hand, I consider making salad, changing the order of the day from its forward movement into a picture I still have of what I used to desire. What I used to desire is among those things that snag and pull me or make me stop. I used to offer Eric every delighted notion—this apple, a kind touch, a chase through dawn light, vaporous and white—that I would have wanted for myself and wanted to give to him. But I don't offer anything to Granger. Instead, I watch him. And this makes me give up the idea of the five of us, my sons and I and Granger and Catherine, sitting down later to a well-prepared dinner, talking over messy plates, sipping hot orange tea as twilight moves through the curtains until features are indistinguishable, until Joey jumps up to flick the light on so it floods us and separates us again from our soft voices. Yes, I abandon that, idea and intent, but it doesn't make me adult and independent. It makes me vicious, and I slam the window down hard enough to rattle the pane, but not hard enough to crack the glass.

Joey comes in and sits across from Catherine, his face sober and confused. I think his entire name, but all I say is, *Hello.* I ignore his glance at Granger. Joey has to be an invisible boy tonight, happy with his brother and the television.

The ring of the phone splits the room into four separate parts. I walk between the others, Granger by the sink, Catherine and Joey at the table, as if there are wires there on the floor. My bare feet feel good on the cool tile.

In her scratchy, Dutch-accented voice, Sheila tells me it's the equinox, and Pat is getting out of jail, so she's having a party. I relay the details to Catherine as I hear them, leaving Granger to listen if he wants.

This is fine, I think, getting Joey to run down to the store and pick out whatever he wants for dinner. Frozen pizza will be okay for once. Joey smiles, and the back of my head gets warmer and lighter than the beer made it feel. Joey goes out happy with ten dollars in his pocket. Catherine wanders next door to use Paul's shower and to explain our change of plans.

About twice a week, Paul tells Catherine he's in love with her. He admires her neat house, her yellow kitchen, her lace curtains. These things bore Catherine; she does not want to be liked for them. Paul, who has been known to threaten suicide, believes Catherine is cheerful and stable. He is suffering through the loss of everything he had except his house, Catherine says, the best way he can manage. Once in a while I invite him over for dinner. He is nice to Joey and David in a distant way, which is fine with me.

Granger is in the shower when Joey gets back, laden with treats in large paper bags. I watch him unpacking, two pop cans in one hand deftly stuck in the fridge door, pizza boxes in the freezer, chips overhead in the cupboard. His skin is very fine; he is too thin. When he turns and says *Mom?* all I can do is put my hand on the wall and lean there until he has finished putting everything away.

As soon as we are inside the highrise building where Sheila lives, we drift apart, and our voices become louder as if to make up for it. It's almost nine o'clock but it's still light. Outside, the building looks okay, but there are half-full green garbage bags in the hall, the lobby glass is broken and taped over, and the elevator, when it comes, is smeared with lipstick and shit. Granger pushes the button for the eleventh floor. Paul stands gingerly gazing at the lighted-up numbers.

EQUINOX

I walk along the hallway, stepping over things, examining the numbers on the doors, and finally knock. Sheila's place is full of people, and Granger and Catherine take the beer we brought into the kitchen.

Sheila let some other man move in with her while Pat was in jail. Pat is on the floor with his legs stretched out in front of him, slumped a bit, smoking with concentration what I guess is one of his first real cigarettes after weeks of roll-your-owns. Sheila walks around the room holding onto the new boyfriend's elbow, introducing him to people.

Granger is on the balcony talking to a woman with freckled shoulders. He looks good out in the open air against the last of the light; shiny, brand new, like an appliance just out of its box.

I'd like to say that watching his hand slide across her back and under her camisole strap doesn't bother me, but the fact is that it always makes me wonder when a man I just got out of bed with a few hours ago can't remember if it happened or not. Or when every gesture seems intended as emotional Spanish fly. I am being unfair. I could look at something else—tall grey apartment towers, totemic, expressionless, with the great red-gold ball of the sun hanging low in the sky behind them. Maybe I want Granger to love me, even though I don't love him. It might be better than that; I might really want us both to love each other, enough so that we might try to figure out what we are doing some of the time.

I go over and kneel close to Pat on the floor, and take a big swallow from the bottle of Jack Daniel's Pat has beside him. I'd forgotten how nice Pat smells, of tobacco and also of something like flowers.

I say, *It's nice to see you*, and we hug without touching very much.

Pat takes my hand and we sit like that for a long time, drinking now and again from the bottle on the floor that reflects all the gold light in the room. I stroke the inside of Pat's forearm and remember Granger telling me that people have been killed near city construction sites: a nurse on her way to St. Mike's had her skull smashed by a flying brick; two lawyers were cut in half by a window that fell from a crane on Bay Street.

I had told Granger I wanted to find out how the wrecking ball was operated. I had told him I wanted to see it for myself, and he asked me to come down and watch him work.

There was sun everywhere. I pushed my sticky bangs off my forehead, and watched out the bus window for the pink hoarding Granger had told me about. If I got there at the right time, he said, I'd get to see the whole wall come down.

There were wire-covered holes in the hoarding. I picked one near the centre. The crane ground with a garish noise as it twisted on its base. Granger was in the cab, his neck strained with concentration, his hands on the controls, levers and an overlarge stick shift. Everything was shining and yellow except the huge black iron ball on the end of the steel cable that began to swing as he moved the hoist back and forth. When it hit the wall the first time, about three floors up, the bricks shimmered and barely gave. The fourth time it was as he had said; the wall began to crumble, as if a giant hand inside the building were pushing its way out. A pile of rubble formed at the base, and as Granger swivelled and backed his machine, other men with hardhats and shovels moved in to clear away the debris. I was supposed to wait for him. I can't remember why I turned and found my way back to the bus stop in the heat without saying hello.

I keep holding Pat's hand until my legs are stiff from sitting on the floor, until after it is dark outside and everyone in the room has moved so much that I have no idea where Catherine or Granger might be. I ask Pat what he's going to do now that he is out of jail, and he squeezes my hand. His eyes close and tears roll down his cheeks.

Pat's sadness hits me in waves. He lived in this apartment before he went to jail. Where will he go now? I am crying too when he says, *Who's that guy who came in with you and Catherine?*

Just Granger, just a friend I sleep with sometimes.

Pat says *A friend you sleep with?* and I don't answer him. The people in the room keep moving and moving. I like the way it makes me dizzy. Paul comes over and gets down on the balls of his feet in front of us like a farmer in a field in a Depression movie. I introduce them and Paul says, *So how was it in jail?* You can tell by the way he asks that it would be the hardest thing in the world for him to imagine what it would be like in jail, no matter what Pat says.

The Jack Daniel's is gone and I have to find a bathroom. People on the balcony are passing a joint; its hot little red eye moves between pinched fingers. I can't see Catherine anywhere, but Granger stops me in the hallway that goes past the bedrooms and puts his hands on the wall behind my head. I hardly know his face. Until this moment I have forgotten what he looks like, and it occurs to me that I will forget again very soon.

He asks if I want to go somewhere and get something to eat. I think it's a good idea, but I want to call

Joey first and check how he and David are doing. The noise level has gone up; people are dancing to wild Latin music. I don't want Joey to hear this. Paul gets involved in our conversation, and borrows the key to another apartment on the same floor as Sheila's. The apartment belongs to a man who is a black shape wobbling with several others on the balcony. Somebody out there yells, and the sound echoes; moving heads lean over the edge of the railing, look out into the void that separates them from other, identical, buildings, that men use their lives putting up and then destroying.

Paul leads me out into the messy, quiet hallway, where the dim greyness is cheerful because it is so uncomplicated. He has bottles of beer from Sheila's fridge in the pockets of his jacket, and we walk slowly, accompanied by the sound of clinking glass.

As soon as the heavy door to the stranger's apartment wheels shut behind us, I phone Joey and hear him say that he's fine. Paul has switched all the lights out, and the chain is on the front door. We sit on the stranger's couch together in the middle of the stranger's things, drinking and watching the curtains drift in on a good strong breeze.

Paul twists the top off another bottle of beer and tells me he had several affairs while his wife's parents were dying of cancer in the hospital. Both of them. He says he saw parallels, he saw death overtaking him the whole time. *I couldn't imagine having sex with only one woman for the rest of my life,* he says seriously. *Not then. But now I can.*

Couldn't, couldn't, couldn't, I think. Paul doesn't say affairs, either, he says, *sex with a lot of women.*

How long have you been divorced? I ask.

Two years.

What's she doing now?

She moved in with a dope addict who races motorcycles for a living.

Hmm, I say.

He comes to me for a hug. I stand up and lead him, feeling my way across the cluttered living room into the kitchen. I fill my empty beer bottle with cold tap-water in the dark.

Tell me about it, I say.

I don't know how it happens. I can't imagine why I go to bed with him. As soon as I am sure he is asleep, I quietly pull on my clothes, take the chain off the door, and leave the apartment unlocked behind me. A number of possibilities go through my mind, like finding Granger's car, if it's still in the parking lot, and curling up in the back seat until he and Catherine decide it's time to go home. And I wonder who Joey will resemble when I get there.

MANY MOTHERS

O N E

◆ Once the government rerouted the highway around Atherly in order to take a bend out, the main street, King, was more or less deserted. Half the cars passing through were lost; the other half were heading somewhere else. Atherly's six motels, built on posts sunk into blasted rock just outside of town, were closed. Faded signs invited motorists to stop and rest; no one had bothered to board up the broken windows facing the water. Even the pretty lake didn't draw tourists, which Aunt Sally said was a shame. Cellie's mother disagreed. She said it was nice to have the rocks and beach to themselves.

Cellie licked the last bit of ice from her lime popsicle and tasted wood. She listened as the two women talked over tea. Her mother's spoon, stirring sugar into a china cup, Aunt Sally's knife, laid back on the plate after buttering a piece of sourdough bread, did not make a sound. Cellie finished her popsicle and wiped her sticky fingers in the grass.

It would be eleven years before Cellie's mother vanished in the dark green waters of the lake.

Princesses, golden thimbles, castles and trolls: strange things happened in stories before the prince and princess could be married and live happily ever after. Cellie's mother had taught her to read, and she sounded out the words lying on her plain white bed, alone in her room. For hours at a time, she pored over the drawings of pink lace dresses and diaphanous fairies.

Cellie trailed her hand along the rough cement wall beside the stairs that led down to the root cellar, tugged the cellar door open by the cool iron handle and stepped into darkness. The cellar smelled of soil and apples and potatoes where they kept preserves on shelves and salt pork hanging. They were poor, her mother said, but the vegetable garden at the back of the yard where the light was good would feed them for most of the winter.

Cellie was checking the cellar for treasure. As far as she could tell, taking flat testing steps across the dirt floor in the dimness, the packed earth beneath her feet was undisturbed. She wanted a treasure, and she wanted to be able to tell the story of her mother. Cellie knew that her mother had ridden a white horse as a girl. She had worn a crown as a singing princess on stage, and wings once when she played an angel. Her mother had walked in her sleep. But there weren't any answers in the dark, and Cellie shut the door carefully against the heat before returning to the yard at the top of the stairs.

Yellow sunlight chopped through the trees in slanted afternoon beams. Apart from the pleasant voices of the women drifting from the kitchen, it was quiet. Cellie's sneakered toes poked over the edge of the back verandah as she arranged white and red and black and brown stones on the wide wooden railing, stones the colours of women's hair and warm as live things in the summer heat. Over the course of many trips to the lake, Cellie had carefully fished the stones from shallow water near the shore, then dried them in the sun and polished them with a cloth. The stones she saved had the shapes of heads and nebulous faces carved into their hard surfaces by time and beating water. She told stories to the stones; she whispered to the tiny head in her palm. It glowed with the vermilion of poppies, of sorcerers' hats and velvet shoes. Cellie loved her mother; she loved to be outside by herself while her mother's voice floated through the wood-framed screen door. As she spoke to the little stones, her miniature mothers, and picked them up one by one to see if they had anything to say, she felt greedy and guilty: why did she want so many mothers when she had such a good one already? Cellie's right hand made the red stone nod.

All around her, white fences edged the rectangular backyards belonging to her house and to her neighbours'. Her mother's garden shimmered in the hot and rising air, orange tiger lilies and blue delphiniums, bleeding hearts and purple flowering chives, nasturtiums and lily of the valley. The clipped grass was flawless. Cellie replaced the red stone beside the others on the railing. A flapping sound, as of sheets whipping in the wind, made her stiffen and search the backyard for its source.

An enormous black bird with a green breast and a yellow beak tottered on top of the fence above her mother's pink roses. Its ungainly body leaned backwards at the same time as its neck curled forward, awkwardly pointing its head down to gaze into the rosebushes. The bird gathered itself and flung its body stupidly off the fence-top and into her yard. After some rustling, it struggled out of the roses and heaved itself onto the grass, where it stumbled, blinking and disoriented. Mesmerized, Cellie knocked her stones with her arm, and they fell off the railing, clicking. The bird's scaly black feet stopped. Its curved beak opened, its breast feathers shivered. The bird's beady glass-yellow eyes, fixed on Cellie in alarm, demanded that she stay back; it waddled, clumsily and wheezing with effort, in front of the verandah and into the patch of Michaelmas daisies on the other side of the lawn. Cellie watched the bird lunge part way out of the daisies, squawking. It hurled its huge body into the air three times, its lustrous green breast swelling with each breath, stumpy black wings batting furiously, before it surged up onto the fence. The bird jumped down into Aunt Sally's yard and out of Cellie's sight, but she could hear its feathers and its legs ferrying it away.

Cellie scrambled down the wooden steps from the verandah to the grass and hurried to the edge of the flower bed where the bird had blundered up out of the daisies. Trembling, Cellie leaned to straighten a stalk with serrated leaves the bird had damaged in its escape. The slatted white fence was too high for her to climb, and though she pushed the leaves and branches eagerly aside, the garden plants were too thickly clustered to see through. Cellie desperately wanted to find out where the bird was going, but by the time she had circled her house and stood peering over the gate into Aunt Sally's yard, the bird had disappeared.

In the spring Cellie and her mother often hiked beside the lake to gather strawberries. Her mother made tarts and preserves to trade for eggs, butter and milk. Cellie had to be careful not to step on the soft fruit sprouting in the dampness underfoot and to leave the hard, white, bitter fruit to ripen. Later, there were raspberries on long prickly canes that whipped her skin; but Cellie's favourites were the fat blueberries that sprang out of the spindly grey-green bushes growing over the rocks.

One afternoon, they were out in their white cotton hats, picking blueberries into large metal buckets—Cellie, her lips and chin and fingers stained bluish-purple, trying not to eat more than she kept—when a man and a woman came up from the lakeshore and walked over the mossy rocks toward them, holding hands. The strangers' clothes were wet, and they moved as if they were blind, free hands extended a little in front of them. They did not wave or speak, but headed silently, dripping, toward Cellie and her mother. Cellie stood up to say hello, but her mother grabbed Cellie's hand and hastily pulled her and their clanking buckets through the sumac brush toward the road.

Death had taken Cellie Becker's father young and his flattened face gazed out from frames on side-tables and on the wall, constant and happy. Cellie's mother wore a plain black dress on Sundays when they walked to church. Dave was always gone, but her mother was a kind of portable heaven: she was either there, making tea and rice pudding with cinnamon and raisins,

MANY MOTHERS

humming—or not there. Her mother could quite easily kneel in the living room, cutting lemon-coloured wool according to a printed pattern, her angular dark head bent over the scissors, and not be there at all.

Cellie's story of her mother began, *Once upon a time in a city far from here* ... but Cellie knew only fragments of her mother's life, and when she tried to string them together into a story they didn't make sense. How did Cellie fit in the part about her mother meeting Dave, her father, when he tried to steal her mother's dog? Or at least her mother thought that he was trying to steal her dog, but really he was getting back on the hockey bus because he played hockey for a living, and the dog liked him and followed him up the bus steps and made the other players laugh. On winter Saturday nights, if Aunt Sally was visiting, her mother let Cellie stay up late and watch hockey on television. It confused her, not least because Cellie had some ideas about things dead people did from her occasional evening talks with Aunt Sally. The dark little men on the ice reminded her of fish in water, and Cellie also thought they might be ghosts of her father; sometimes she suspected that one or another of the hockey players waved to her with a tiny dark hand.

Cellie coughed and coughed. *Get it out of your system,* her mother said patiently. Cellie stood up and coughed, curled in a ball on the floor and coughed until a sharper pain drove from her throat into her chest. Her room smelled of toast, medicinal syrup and damp heat. Beside the bed, on a white cane chair, her mother sat wringing a washcloth with cool water in a basin. When Cellie stopped coughing, her mother helped her into bed and tucked the sheets around her shoulders. She smoothed back Cellie's bangs and softly folded the cloth against her hot forehead.

Cellie had a nightmare. A bird the size of her mother climbed up out of the lake. It could not fly because of the thin mud soaked into its wings. The bird stumbled across the ground, eating pennies and pieces of paper with writing on them. Cellie could see that the bird's craw was swollen with the things it had taken in its beak, and when it swallowed she began to cry.

The evil stepmother or old witch was missing from her mother's story, and Cellie asked if Aunt Sally was an evil old witch. Her mother sputtered, *Evil old witch?* and snapped off a stem of the arum ivy she was re-potting. Cellie persisted: did her mother know any old witches? Had one perhaps been lingering about when Dave died? Her mother replied that Dave had had enough old

MANY MOTHERS

witch in himself to do the trick, and that Cellie should go and fetch the hammer from downstairs so they could put up the hooks for the hanging plants.

Cellie's mother unfolded the ironing board in the sewing room and sighed and punched her hands deep into her pockets. Cellie was holding down a cotton skirt, poking the arrow-shaped tip of the iron into a pleat, when she burned the inside of her forearm. She did not cry, but came into the living room to tell her mother what had happened. Cellie stood holding her arm just above the swelling red mark, and said out loud, *I've burned myself*. She said it again, but her mother, lost in the clipping and slow laying of bits of twig on a newspaper folded on the windowsill, ignored her. Her mother's hands clipped with the scissors. Her mother's body was in the living room, but she was gone. Her mother had disappeared somewhere. Cellie wanted to go, too.

After she stopped reading Cellie fairy tales, Cellie's mother read to her out of whatever fat book was at hand, randomly and at any moment that struck her: over breakfast; in the middle of a walk; while she dusted. Cellie understood very little of what she heard, because now her mother read to her in the same way she told stories about herself: one page from a green book; a funny sentence; all the dialogue from one chapter. But Cellie remembered names—Catherine, Penelope, Mrs. Dalloway—and repeated them to herself. Cellie's mother never said so, but Cellie assumed that she was being read to about other mothers and the places that they went.

Cellie's mother had a first name but Cellie didn't know what it was. Her father was dead and even Aunt Sally called her mother *Mrs. Becker*, just as her mother called Aunt Sally *Miss Arnprior*, because they were not related.

Aunt Sally lived next door with a woman Cellie called Aunt Marjory. Cellie didn't like Aunt Marjory. She made bread and cookies burnt black at the edges or with too little sugar in them or hard as mica on her teeth, but expected Cellie to eat everything on her plate. Aunt Marjory, for some reason, was always trying to rid her yard of squirrels, and could sometimes be seen in her small front garden, hitting the oak tree with a baseball bat.

Occasionally, Aunt Sally came to stay with Cellie when her mother was going out, to a Horticultural Society Meeting, for instance, or to buy a skirt-length from Droozer's. Aunt Sally had a great soft lap, and steel-rimmed spectacles which she allowed Cellie to try on. She wrote historical books, and spoke to the little girl, as her mother did, as if Cellie would understand everything she heard. Aunt Sally was very fond of ghosts and foreign ideas about the dead. She also would drink a glass of sherry after dinner, and sometimes two or three more glasses after Cellie's mother went out, which made her talkative, and her voice as sweet and fuzzy as the smell of her breath. Aunt Sally was writing a book about the lake and the settlements around it. The book's first chapter, Aunt Sally said, concerned the wreck of the Marsupial, a ferry which for some years had run across the channel from Atherly to an island at the north end of the lake.

One of the things about our lake, Aunt Sally told her, *is that there is a lot of sand in it, and the sand drifts and piles under water into new shapes which sometimes get in the way of boats and can sink them if they run aground and tip; the bottom has to be constantly re-charted. The day the Marsupial went down, my sister was crossing with her fiancé and a crowd of others for a holiday picnic. It was gorgeous weather,* Aunt Sally said, *much like today. I can't remember why I wasn't with them, although I was probably wearing trousers and strutting about being disdainful of their fun. You can imagine the lovely dresses and hats,* Aunt

Sally said. *A lot of us on the shore were still waving when the ferry tilted to one side and water poured over the railings—the people on deck got wet and began to scream and wave and cry. For a moment—things always look closer over water than they are—I believed that they would all come swimming back, even as the ferry's bow sank under the waves—anything else with the hot sun shining down seemed impossible. It was several minutes before the rowboats and whatever else was at hand could be launched and hauled by oar or sail across the water to rescue whoever was still afloat, my sister among them, bless her, though it was hard to make sense in the scramble, or even to be grateful when they were already dragging for bodies. Eleven women drowned in their long dresses.* Aunt Sally squinted at the shadows thrown by the lamp in Cellie's living room. *Once I went to the beach late at night, and a man and a woman in party clothes dripping with weeds walked right up out of the depths of the lake, soaked in black mud and green bottom slime from hair to shoes.* Aunt Sally sipped her sherry and looked appraisingly at Cellie. *They were followed out of the water by others, who crooked their muddy fingers and tried to call me to join their party, but they could not talk. When they opened their mouths, black water bubbled out.*

On a windy day in May, Cellie and her mother were hanging the old linens out to air on the line in the backyard: quilts and embroidered pillow cases and creamy woollen blankets normally stored in a cedar-lined closet upstairs and rarely used. Cellie's mother informed her that she had decided to marry again, and that Cellie was soon going to meet the man who would be coming to live with them. Her mother said the man was named Dave, like her father, and she seemed to find the coincidence curious, though it was hard for Cellie to be sure because her mother's mouth was full of clothespins. Cellie handed her the next thing in the wicker basket, a white lace table cloth large enough for their dining-room table with the three extra leaves in. Her mother shook out its folds, checking for stains or holes. The cloth hung down to her feet like a long white skirt, then gathered up in the wind, covering Cellie's mother in lace, blowing completely over her body so it appeared that only her mother's form remained, her face masked by the white cloth under which she had disappeared. Her mother stood still for what seemed a long time, and the only sounds were of wind and the linens on the line flapping. Panic welled up in Cellie—the multi-coloured rocks she had knocked off the railing and forgotten lay scattered on the grass below. With a dreadful and clumsy slowness, she reached over and pulled at the cloth; her fingers trembled as the white stuff fell away, unveiling her mother's face. A face that was only smiling.

When Dave moved in (as Cellie thought, *again*) life became big and noisy and the house had cigarette smoke in it and voices echoed in the rooms day and night. Pictures of Cellie's father disappeared from their gilt frames on the piano and on the nightstand in her mother's room, and chairs and cabinets were painted brighter colours, as if Dave's loudness coated and changed everything. He seemed oddly familiar—the way he held a hammer, yelled at the dog he bought for her, rubbed his chin coming out of the bathroom after shaving. Cellie assumed that the soul of her father had been transferred into Dave. Her father's soul had been preserved, waxy and waiting, until it could be brought back to life. The front door banged abruptly and sent one or another of them into or out of the house, and Cellie forgot about stories and the pieces that were missing from them for a while.

TWO

Once the government began dredging the sandy harbour-bottoms regularly, boat and tourist traffic in and around the town increased. Deep and treacherous at its centre, the long lake at Atherly is situated where weather systems cross. Steamy air from the southwest and icy air from the north mix to create storms that are exaggerated by their containment within high shores that are mainly cliffs and rock. Bad weather strikes swiftly; low bushes on the islands move like animals, tall pines tremble and sway in roaring gales. Slicing wet winds churn the green-black water into waves that surge ten feet in height, whitecaps topped with foam like lace blown off a clothesline. The empty blue sky fills with purple-brown cumulonimbus and grey rain pours down.

During such a storm, Dave's cabin cruiser capsized and Cellie's mother disappeared into the lake. Her body was lost. The police told Cellie a man in a boat nearby had tried to shout a warning as he made ready to get back to shore when the storm hit. The man heard voices over the water, a man and a woman screaming, and had just got his motor started when waves crashed over their bow and the keel poked up where the cabin had just been. The police found Dave's little boat three days later, aground on the shore of a lagoon north of town. They drove Cellie there to identify the wreck. She stood trembling in the thistles and Queen Anne's lace, while a blue arm held back a hawthorn branch so she could see water licking at the broken hull.

Cellie lives by herself, in a small upstairs room in a boarding house where the dinner dishes are thick, the lilacs painted on them years before faded by hot dishwater. A place is set for her at the table whether she eats in the dining room or not. She has an iron bed, a bookshelf, and a tinny radio.

Perspiring in the August heat behind the counter at Packham's Drugs where she works as a sales clerk, Cellie sighs. Sunlight chops through orange and red and yellow and brown bottles high on shelves near the window and reflects on the skin of her arms.

She watches the flat black and white clock on the wall and unlocks the front door of the drugstore from the inside, the way she does every morning, Monday to Friday. She counts change with an inattentive care born of repetition, and plunks it into the slots in the open till before she clangs the cash drawer shut. With vinegar and water and crumpled paper towels, she wipes down the front window. She rubs the glass hard and scrapes at a wedge of dirt in the corner of the wooden frame.

From here Cellie can see Atherly's entire downtown, the coloured awnings and the quiet stores, the nearly empty street where nothing seems to change except the weather and the mood of the lake.

A number of women in Atherly look like Cellie Becker's mother, and it hurts Cellie to see them with their paper bags of oranges and hamburger, their dry limber walk going in the other direction, like ghosts of her mother leaving her alone. Once when she was very small, she straggled far behind her mother on the sidewalk. She yelled Mommy! and many women stopped, their cardigans and flowered skirts swinging as they turned; their troubled eyes studied her in concern.

At about ten o'clock a woman with straight shoulders gets off the northbound local bus. The woman's black hair is arranged in a loose chignon. Awkwardly, as if it weighs a great deal, she slings an overnight bag of good cowhide up onto the slatted wooden bench that serves as the bus stop. Underneath a black cloth raincoat, she is wearing a green dress.

It is a funny thing for anyone to get off the local bus at the downtown crossing. Cellie Becker, behind the cash register rolling dull copper pennies into paper wrappers, watches the woman peer up and down the street, blinking and disoriented. Still wearing her raincoat, the woman sits on the bench and opens a book as if she were in her own living room.

Across the street, a shadow passes on the white brick wall and disappears.

Cellie squints at the glare and pulls a glossy travel magazine out of the rack to her right. Her hot fingers stick to photographs of white horses, of red skiffs drawn up on sand, of old stone roads and minarets and widows in black veils.

It is shadowy and hot inside the drugstore, airless and silent except for the rippling of ribbons on a small fan humming at the back. Water beads on the panels of the cooler and falls soundlessly onto the wooden floor.

Wishing that the woman would come and buy a treat and give her someone to talk to, Cellie wanders back between the shelves of skin cream, aspirin, and rubber gloves to the pop cooler. She plunges her right hand into the ice and holds it there until cold aches in the small bones of her wrist. She runs her wet palm around the back of her neck under her hair.

A little after eleven o'clock, Mrs. Packham bustles in so that Cellie can take her break. After glancing out to make sure the woman is still on the bench, Cellie hurries to the cooler and scoops up a can of cola and a bottle of grapefruit juice. She presents Mrs. Packham with a two dollar bill and taps her fingernails on the counter.

It isn't any hotter outside than it was in the store, despite the round white sun overhead. Air moving off the lake rustles the dry leaves of junipers planted along the boulevard. Black spots appear on the sidewalk where condensation from the cold drinks drips into the dust.

MANY MOTHERS

Holding out the bottle of grapefruit juice, Cellie stops in front of the woman, who is about Aunt Sally's age. Her yellow, pointy face, bent over her book, is framed with shiny black hair. A curious verdant colour, her dress is finely tailored; her tiny feet, laced tightly into black boots, tap the sidewalk as she reads. Cellie clears her throat.

I saw you sitting here, Cellie says, *and I thought you might want a cold drink.*

Fixed on Cellie, the woman's dark eyes squint before she sets her book aside and reaches up with crooked bony fingers for the bottle. Cellie goes on:

My name is Cellie Becker and I work at Packham's Drugs over there—she points—*which is why I know you've been out in the heat since the bus left. I lost my mother in that lake,* she says, plunking herself beside the woman on the bench and opening her can of pop with a sharp fizz. The woman unscrews the cap on the bottle and sips, her thin lips puckered as if she finds the taste very strange.

Cellie asks the woman her name. She says, abruptly, *Betty Smith*, edging down the bench away from Cellie, her eyes hooded, lines deepening around her mouth. But Cellie is pleased and replies that it is a very nice name and sounds English, and what is she doing in Atherly?

As Betty Smith hesitates, hot wind rises from the west, riffling the bright banners and flags in the square, teasing the leaves on the silver maples white and green. A small girl throws a stick over the grass and a fat grey dog ambles after it.

I fell in love with a monk out west, Betty says finally. *He didn't love me enough to leave the order. It was what I expected,* she continues, scrutinizing Cellie's face as if she needs to believe that Cellie would have foreseen tragedy, too. *But I didn't think I'd be so devastated.*

Where out west?

Nantikokan, British Columbia, the woman says, *the most beautiful valley in the world. Maybe it was the place I loved really, and not him. You're very sweet,* she adds, patting Cellie's wrist.

Have you been to a lot of places? Cellie asks.

Oh, yes, says Betty Smith, *I've been all over Canada and lived for two years in Moscow. I travelled with the circus at that time; sold fried fish beside the Rhone; spied for the Luddites; ended up doing translations for the government. I learned fluent Czech and Portuguese in Paris, and a smattering of Chinese at the embassy. But my stay with the Inuit on the Antarctic Islands is what I treasure most. I had a radio show,* she says, her voice loud and scratchy as a quill on rough paper. *I lived with a harpist, and we spent our summers doing research for the program, down by the* ocean measuring walruses and penguins and observing their habits. He died though, of tuberculosis, and so I took the next boat back to Montreal. *That was a sad time.* She closes her eyes.

Water and asphalt glisten in front of Cellie and the woman in the still and silent heat. Betty Smith is speaking in another language now, fast and close and mesmerizing, her old hands gesturing, extended a little in front of her. Shimmering clear waves float in the air; the storefronts across the square appear to alternately melt and harden.

Finally Cellie notices Mrs. Packham under the awning in front of the drugstore window, waving. As she gets up to go, Cellie sees tears in Betty's eyes.

Cellie spends the rest of the afternoon at the counter in the drugstore, looking at the lake. She watches Betty gather her bag and hurry up the steps of the southbound bus, the green front of her dress strained by the long handle of the bag pulling on her shoulder. Her coat is buttoned at the neck and draped loosely like a cape, and its black arms flap as she disappears. Through the bus windows Cellie can see the heads of women, women with red and black and white and brown hair, some of whom look like her mother. Cellie spends the entire afternoon realizing and accepting what she has decided to do, how she will go toward wherever it was her mother often seemed to be before the story went wrong and she was drowned, how she will have to study and scrimp and save and that it will all be extremely difficult. She will not announce her plans until she is ready to leave. Could she explain, for instance, to Mrs. Packham, that a woman named Betty Smith sat beside her on a park bench and, in only an hour, made the rest of the world absolutely real?

THREE MONTHS

◆ Ida met Cullen on a bus that was going north from Bloor along Bathurst Street. It was neither a sunny nor a fine day. It was an October day in Toronto. That winter was coming barely seemed possible: the trees were haggard but holding their leaves and the clouds were still broken and white. Coats were cheap in the stores. Ida looked through the bus window and saw rows of yellow rubber boots on a wooden table outside. BARGAIN! the red sign said: PLUSH-LINED!

The bus slumped to a stop and Ida's bag slipped onto the floor. A man who was standing bent down to pick it up but she already had the bag in her hand and he smiled apologetically. The bus had become crowded and Ida realized she was taking up two seats. She moved over so that he could sit down.

Ida looked up the aisle of the bus at the garish ads and the variously coloured heads swaying like the tops of brown weeds. She was very bored.

The man cleared his throat. He was thin and clean, but rumpled looking. He had curly black hair and wore glasses. He said, 'Hardly anyone knows about that bookstore.' He pointed from his book bag to hers. He made it sound very intimate that they had both shopped at the same place.

'They always seem to have what I want,' said Ida politely.

'That's exactly it,' he said, completely pleased with himself. 'I do most of my reading at university libraries, but when I need something refreshing, to take my mind off work, that's where I go.'

He turned in the seat. His shoulder touched Ida's shoulder. Ida did not want to look him in the eye. It was hot on the bus. He wanted to keep talking. Ida was not lonely. Ida was bored.

'Are you knitting a sweater, or what?' he asked. Ida closed the fat brown bag on her lap.

'I'm a weaver,' she said. 'This is wool for a length of coating.'

He seemed delighted. He leaned forward and smiled. 'I didn't know urban dwellers still did that by hand.'

Ida shrugged. Her stop was coming up. She stood with her bags and reached carefully over the heads of two giggling women to pull the bell cord. She sidled through the crowd, and when she finally reached the sidewalk, he was right behind her.

'Well,' Ida said, 'this is where I live.'

THREE MONTHS

He grinned and pulled out a brass key. 'I live here, too,' he said.

The clouds had closed over and the sky was tinged with purple. He opened the heavy green door and Ida went ahead, loaded down with her bags. Their temporary alliance was now extending into the hall, and possibly into hellos in the morning, chats at the mailbox. Me and people, thought Ida, never work out.

He was whistling. They both checked their boxes for mail. Ida had some. She turned to go.

'Why don't you take your things up and then come down and have tea with me and Rachel?' he asked.

'Sure,' Ida said, 'in a few minutes.'

'Number seventeen,' he said, 'and don't forget!'

Ida trudged upstairs. Jean had oiled the bannister again and Ida kept away from it.

When Ida had shared a house with Mack, there had been a private room for weaving, with shelves she'd built along the walls. The loom dominated this tiny apartment, and she still wasn't used to the way it took over all the space in the main room with wood or shadows of wood and thread. Her small work table and chairs and the fridge and stove looked like toys in comparison, her cot ridiculous and incapable of supporting her weight. The loom sat under the high old window like a broken-down piano, overwhelming in context but too expensive to throw away. And then the warp she had strung the day before, taut through the heddles; a web. Ida thought about threading the shuttles instead of going downstairs, but it was too late. She had agreed. Ida put a dish of cat food out on the fire escape for Alphie, and took off her shoes. Jean has such clean floors; isn't it a pleasant surprise to find a building so well-kept, she thought she might say to Rachel.

Ida knocked and she heard a woman say, 'Somebody at the door, Cullen, why don't you get it?' and then he was ushering her in and saying very familiarly to Rachel, 'See, I told you she'd come,' and Ida thought maybe they're American or they just do this all the time, having strangers in for tea and so on. The kettle was whistling, and Rachel, who had just popped around the corner, disappeared again, like a shy child who'd just wanted a glimpse of the adults at a party.

There were soapstone carvings everywhere in the room. 'We lived in the Arctic,' said Cullen proudly. He handed Ida a small sculpture of a polar bear. It was soft and smooth and cold. Even though Ida kept it in her hand for a few minutes, the cold would not go away. Cullen was telling her about the struggle between the Inuit and the Quallunaat. He waved his arms while he was talking, describing carvers he had seen, working on the ice, he was proud of everything.

THREE MONTHS

'All white,' he said, 'and pure, and you think maybe for a minute that nothing and nobody will ever happen upon you again, and then a snowmobile, god, it's a relief and it's hell.'

There was almost no light left in the room and Ida walked around with her arms folded under her breasts, leaning over and looking carefully at each of the sculptures. Most of them were small human figures. She didn't touch them. She didn't want to break anything.

'Rachel was teaching up there and she came home crying every night because of the children. Some of them were orphans, half of them had tuberculosis, and the only money to be made was in trapping for the Bay. I wanted her to leave with me, but she stuck out the whole year.' Rachel, visible now in the kitchen from where Ida was standing, smiled at Ida. Ida smiled back.

The kitchen was bright and Rachel said, 'I hope you like camomile tea; I could make you some coffee instead if you want.'

Ida said tea would be fine.

Rachel thought it was wonderful that Ida made a living weaving. She asked if Ida had ever read Hauptmann's *The Weavers*. Ida hadn't. Rachel wanted to see the loom some time, and she wondered if Ida took small commissions because there were some things she'd love to have handmade for the baby. Ida said yes, but she didn't sew anything, she just made the cloth. To change the subject, she marvelled that Rachel was pregnant, beause she couldn't tell. Rachel stood up, she was fairly tall, and showed Ida the profile of her body, pulling her cotton shirt in to accentuate the little bulge at her waist.

'Tiny yet, isn't she?' asked Rachel, and Ida said, well, she didn't know. Cullen got up from the table and took his cup into the other room without saying anything. Ida looked after him, embarrassed. What is he pouting about, she wondered, remembering the brass key in his hand.

Rachel shrugged. 'Do you want some more tea?' she asked.

Rachel's stuck here alone a lot, thought Ida. Maybe Cullen thought I'd make a perfect friend.

Rachel was saying something about Thunder Bay. She and Cullen had met at the university there. 'Cullen got his M.A. summa cum laude there after the Yukon research,' she said.

'So did she, don't let her kid you,' yelled Cullen, from the other room.

'It's been a strange time,' said Rachel. 'Things went so smoothly, moving south—and they accepted Cullen here so easily. He's really very bright and dedicated.'

THREE MONTHS

She made it sound like a job application. Ida stirred her tea.

'Have you ever been up north, Ida? Really up north?' asked Rachel. Ida shook her head. 'Cullen hadn't either, until then,' she said. 'Quite a shock for a well-brought-up city boy. He's been glad to get back.'

Ida smiled, though she noticed Rachel hadn't said she was happy to be here. Rachel had a charming way of talking, with her shoulders and head back; relaxed and on stage at the same time.

'If you're going to get personal, what about the miscarriage as a reason for giving up the fort?' asked Cullen, who was leaning in the doorway.

'Yes,' Rachel said. 'That's true.'

It was past time to go. Ida thanked them very much for the tea.

It was too dark to operate the loom when Ida got back upstairs. Even with the overhead light on, shadows from her hands made it too difficult. No amount of artificial light could untangle the mass of threads and shadow enough so that she could see what she was doing. Ida was angry with herself for missing the light. She opened the fire escape door and put a clean rag in Alphie's box. She forced herself to lay out the skeins of wool on her work table so that she could load the shuttles with thread. The loom hulked against the wall.

Ida caught the thread in a shuttle and had to begin again. She worked slowly, and by the time she had filled three shuttles she was tired enough to sleep.

◆

It was a good time to be working hard, the eight weeks before Christmas. Ida ate vegetarian food for a change, and performed scores of sit-ups on the bare wood floor. She got new commissions and became used to the barrenness of the white-painted apartment, the chalky north wall striated with the loom's black shadow, and enjoyed the way the only real colour came from the wood of the loom and the material rolled up at the back of it. She took advantage of the unseasonably warm sun coming in the big south window to work long hours. She read Mack's letters from Montreal without rancour. Ida decided that she had to accept the way that Mack, without telling her, had sold the furniture and china, everything they owned except the loom, to get the money to go. Mack would repay her, one way or another.

Ida finished the coat-length and began making cloth for a huge white sculpture designed by an artist friend of Mack's. This was the way she worked best, inside someone else's structure. Bent to her work, driving the pedals with her bare feet that forced the loom's working parts

THREE MONTHS

up and down, Ida covered the floor with piles of bone-white cloth.

When Ida was working she was almost happy. The white cloth was a controllable landscape. The heddles went up and down like waves, and rolls of cloth lay at the back of the loom, golden in the winter sunset. Taut threads over the frame stretched away like field furrows slowly being filled in.

Ida did not see people. The winter days were long and cold and the nights were long and cold. Ida wove hundreds of yards of white cloth in twenty-foot pieces. She piled them on the floor when she was done. When she looked up from her work, out the window, she saw the frozen sky and the black edge of the roof next door. It snowed, constantly.

One night, there was a knock at the door. Ida was surprised to see Cullen standing there. The blue dress she was wearing was too tight and her apartment was hot.

'Come in,' said Ida, 'it's cold.' Jean had turned the radiators off in the halls again.

'Are you busy?' asked Cullen.

Ida made coffee and Cullen explained that he wanted to borrow the book she had had with her on the bus.

Ida found the book on the windowsill and handed it to Cullen, but he did not leave. He leaned forward in the kitchen chair she had offered him with the coffee, and talked. The professor overseeing Cullen's work was exacting and professional; he was an angel, in fact; Cullen's graduate students were interested and capable; the facilities were terrific; but Cullen's work was going badly. He did research in the library and came home to find he'd written out totally irrelevant notes. It was like being crazy, Cullen said, thinking you've done one thing and then discovering you've done something entirely different. When Cullen talked he leaned very close, he reached out with his face.

'Sometimes,' he said vaguely, 'I just can't stand it.'

Ida thought she heard Alphie crying outside. 'Did you hear that?' she asked Cullen.

'What?' he said. 'No.'

Alphie clawed the screen of the fire escape door, trying to get Ida's attention. He yowled. Ida went over and opened the door. Holding the cat's head so he wouldn't get in, she retrieved his dish from the snowy black steel landing.

'Is that your cat?' asked Cullen.

'Not really,' said Ida, rinsing the dish in hot water at the sink. 'Someone must have left him behind when they moved. I've just been feeding him.'

THREE MONTHS

'Why don't you let him in?'

Ida pointed at the loom. 'Can you imagine the mess he'd make?'

It became habitual for Cullen to arrive at Ida's door about seven, once or twice a week, armed with pastries. Sometimes Cullen came in and they talked, Cullen perched on the edge of one of Ida's kitchen chairs, his legs crossed, and Ida across the work table from him, leaning back and squinting in the glare from the overhead light.

Ida told Cullen how Mack had been ruined at three different galleries. He could not finish a show on time. Mack owed a huge amount of money to one Toronto gallery for materials. Ida told Cullen that Mack was painting dogs and flowers in Montreal.

Cullen told Ida that he often stood in the stationery store and stared at the file cards. He could not decide between white cards and orange cards. Cullen said it was hard to concentrate with Rachel in the apartment all the time. Rachel and Cullen fought about who could use the typewriter.

One night Cullen came up drunk and late. Ida let him in, and he muttered how sorry he was. His hair was greasy and he ran his hand through it over and over again, leaning forward in his chair. After a while he leaned back and fell asleep and Ida woke him up and sent him home.

Ida was making lots of money and she was not thinking. She worked each day until the light disappeared, and indulged herself in the evening. Ida invited Jean up for a cup of coffee and gave her a bottle of Scotch in case she decided to keep the apartment for a long time.

Ida was not thinking and she was amused by Cullen. She wrote long letters to Mack in Montreal and washed Alphie's rags. She made a piece of soft flannel for Rachel's baby.

Ida dreamed that she and Cullen were making love in the snow, somewhere where there were no buildings. It was cold. They did not seem to be breathing. The wind was moaning and panting instead. There was the sound, not of bodies rubbing or slapping together, but of blocks of ice hitting in a void.

Ida woke up. It was the middle of the night. Someone was pounding on the door. Ida knew it was Cullen. She had lost track of time and wondered if it was New Year's Eve. She climbed out of bed and draped the blankets around her naked body like a cape. She stood in the dark in her bare feet, wondering if she should let Cullen in.

He pounded again, and seemed to wait; then he lunged at the door. The door trembled but did not give. Ida could see the crack of light beside the hinges change shape. Go away, she whispered, but it didn't work; Cullen was yelling and Ida was sad. He must be very drunk, she thought, he must be. He said, 'Ida, let me in.' Ida stood wrapped in her blankets, shivering. 'Rachel hates me,' he said, 'I punched her in the stomach. Up north,' he said, 'I punched her.'

Ida got back into bed and pulled the covers up around her neck. She listened until Cullen went away.

◆

Ida got a letter from Mack. Happy New Year, it said, come and visit. Come and stay, if you want. Mack was selling his saleable realism to happy rich people from Westmount. Bring samples, Mack said, I've got lots of new friends.

Ida packed. She soaked in a hot bath. She phoned the airport and a cab. She could come back for the loom, or buy another.

She stopped at Rachel and Cullen's door on the way downstairs. She had Rachel's cloth in one hand. Ida knocked on the door.

Rachel opened it. She looked at Ida's suitcase but not at her face. Cullen was sitting on the chesterfield, reading. Rachel looked more pregnant.

Rachel left Ida standing in the doorway and walked over to the couch where Cullen was sitting. She tapped Cullen on the knee.

'Ida's here,' she said.

Cullen did not look up.

'Where are you going, Ida?' Rachel asked.

'Montreal,' said Ida. She wanted to say something else. She wanted to tell Rachel that she had not let him in. But all she said was, 'I just stopped to say goodbye. And to give you this cloth for the baby, if you want it.'

Rachel came back to the doorway and took the cloth from Ida's hand. Ida smelled gin on Rachel's breath.

Rachel clutched the material. 'It's nice,' she said to Ida, 'thanks.'

The soapstone sculptures on the shelves and tables, all the stone things in the room were in the same places as they had been before. Stone men and stone women wrapped in coats made of stone.

'Cullen, did you hear that?' Rachel asked. She cocked her head to one side and wandered unsteadily toward the couch. Cullen read more intently. Rachel

THREE MONTHS

went to the window and peeked out, then opened the fire escape door.

'Oh, it's Ida's cat,' Rachel said. She picked Alphie up and brought him, hanging limply from her hands, into the warmth. Ida was sure she could hear Alphie purring. 'Nice kitty,' Rachel said, rubbing her chin on Alphie's head and half-wrapping him in Ida's white cloth. 'Good little boy.'

'Cullen, can we keep him?' Rachel said. 'Nice puss.'

'Get rid of it,' Cullen said, without looking up.

Ida picked up her suitcase and walked along the hallway. She pressed open the front door of the building with her shoulder, and stood outside on the stone steps, breathing the icy air.

Ida waited for the cab. She gripped her bag in one hand. Grey light seeped down through the clouds, and grey snow covered the lawn beside the stairs. The sidewalk had been cleared. Only in the snowbanks along the curb, where people had climbed over to cross the street, were there traces of footsteps.

BLACK BRANCH IN YELLOW WIND

◆ The television hangs from a hook in the corner. Danka turns up the sound. We are waiting for X to come back with a bottle of wine.

I was married to X for eight years. We now live separately. Outside it is raining. My black bicycle, which has been stolen twice and twice recovered, will be soaked.

I ask Danka if I can buy the painting and go, but Danka insists that X wants the same one, the portrait of a baby's head, and that I should wait. Danka's eyes are closed.

X is a historian who specializes in the rebellions of 1837. When he writes he tends to force his pen down through the paper, and when this happens he looks up over his shoulder to see if anyone has noticed. X is good with plants, bad with animals. When X stands in the doorway of my room, his arms reach up to the top of the door frame as if he were stretched on a rack, and I can't see his fingers.

Several of Danka's paintings are gone from the wall

of his apartment. I ask him what happened to them. Barely parting his lips to let the word out, he says, *Sold*. I do not understand how his models can endure having their images separated from their bodies and then disappearing.

Earlier in the afternoon, X and Danka had talked for hours while I worked in a corner, transcribing an interview, using Danka's tape recorder. Their voices rose and fell, and then Danka's voice became loud and resentful. About X's mouth, a slight twitch, then. I also felt my face tighten. Was Danka trying to make X and I think about what we were giving up?

I want to grab the collar of Danka's shirt and rip it open. I want him to move, to be alive. Nodding, he reminds me of my sister Toby with her prison kitten look, her eyes empty, my idiot sister with her soft flat feet and now grey hair. As soon as you see the prisoner with a kitten in the movie you know something is going to happen to it. But Toby is safe. Nothing has ever happened to Toby that a cup of hot chocolate couldn't fix. I stare at Danka and his paintings stare back at me.

My father was a photographer who took portraits for a living. From behind the door sometimes, my crinoline crushed against the wood, I watched him bribing

BLACK BRANCH IN YELLOW WIND

children into a happy glow before he snapped a permanent record of their visit to his studio. The paying mother clapped her hands, the children on the banquette grinned at them both. My tall father would eventually lead his temporary family out through the hall, an elegant replaceable fixture, smiling broadly until the door was shut behind them and he turned the music on.

At this point in the day, I am in love with Roland Barthes, who said, *It fades and fades and fades.* Barthes also said, *I am in mourning for an object which is itself in mourning.*

X returns, smoking a joint, his red hair plastered to his white forehead, his leather jacket darker brown where it is wettest. I have nearly decided to try and talk to X about the man in the black coat, but when I see his half-closed bloodshot eyes, I put on my red mackintosh and slide past him on the stairs without speaking.

Fine, I think, borrowing Danka's umbrella from the brass stand in the vestibule.

I open the umbrella and create a small black sky under the rain. Fine, I think, balancing the umbrella while I unlock my bike and begin to walk it beside me. The tires whisper with water from the sidewalk. Bright storefronts line the street.

I stop and turn inside the rustling crowd moving quickly through the wet. I am sure I have seen the man in the black coat, his arrested step, his damp hand and black sleeve reaching up to shield his face.

One of my first memories is of being aware of my tongue, a long few minutes when it was strangely large in the hollow between my teeth, when the tip had to curl up to fit. With my tongue so big I couldn't speak to explain what was happening in my mouth. I was in a park with my father, and I wanted to tell him. He silently handed me two waffles dripping with vanilla ice cream, but I did not open my lips to bite.

The arm in its black sleeve arcs through the aura of yellow light perpetually. It does not waver like a branch in a strong wind, or mechanically lift like the arm of a motorized crane. Somehow it feels wrong (though 'wrong' is not the word); it feels deceptive to imagine myself in lives other than my own, even though that life is reduced and concentrated into this one recurrent moment. Some evenings, when the light is that way, but not every night it is that way, I have a glass of brandy, or two glasses. But it is not every night and so I am relieved. What would I want with other lives? With the exception of that moving arm, I can live with

BLACK BRANCH IN YELLOW WIND

myself and with what I am—my love of worn, cracked dishes, my artless eating and black clothes, my reading and occasional impulsive trips away.

When I left X, I moved into a room at Bloor and Bathurst. He comes to visit. He speaks to me; his arms in their leather sleeves reach up so that his hands rest on the top of the door frame. I watch his sweet lips glistening against his teeth.

People kill their own children all the time, X says, apropos of nothing. X and I never wanted a child, foreseeing, perhaps, moments like these. *A man threw his young son out of a moving car on the highway*, X says. *A mother wrapped her baby in plastic as soon as it was born in a gas station washroom. Surely*, X says, *surely you can see what I'm trying to tell you.*

No, I say to him. *No, I don't really.*

He stands there while I make orange juice and look at the colour of it.

I unlock my green wooden door one day and find my things disarranged. Something is missing. The window is open and the curtains move like men in business suits.

Light glows in folds of black fabric at the elbow, threatening and pacifying, abridging yellow and staining it, marking and remarking like a knife in butter, a log in floodwater. Antiphonic, always away from the centre, but never into other lives, I am safely endangered again and again.

It is dark and X stands in the open doorway. The lights in my room are turned off, and he is outlined there, his face invisible.
Don't you remember, he says, when you and I swam naked at that big rock quarry outside Paris and the sun was beating down on us like industrial music and the air was warm and we were soaking wet lying on the sand and you kept sitting up but your hair didn't quite cover your breasts until we were dry?
No, I say to him. *No, I don't remember.*

I soothe my hot face with a thick white towel.
Steaming water that smells of sulphur pours from the shower head into the tub. Water rushes down into the hole in the enamel like something dreamed and racing. The telephone rings and rings.

That minute when we knew Toby was missing again, the snow fell like clouds of white locusts against midnight-blue air, we immediately dressed in heavy coats and boots and moved beyond the door, the fence, to find her wandering bewildered two streets away, the elemental quiet and the smell of chicken and lemon in the house when we returned, and

Every relationship means terror and the calm gaze of a statue. I do not, for instance, drink orange juice standing near the desk covered with papers, although I do drink orange juice standing beside the window.

Just a painting of a baby's head, a small baby lying down with white in the background, little fists clutched above its shoulders, a yellow sweater with flat bone buttons. Is there a rattle or a doll clutched in one of the baby's painted hands? I can't remember.

X stands in the doorway and says, *Do you remember the time I chalked a circle on the sidewalk while you stood for ten minutes looking at the fish and birds in Woolworth's? How I'd hoped you wouldn't mind, that I had this incredible attack of anomie standing there?*

I go and ask Danka about the painting again, but he puts me off. He has taken it down from the wall. Did X already buy it? Perhaps Danka doesn't want to sell the painting after all. He seems glad to see me, and offers coffee or a glass of beer, keeping his head bent over the slanted table where he sketches. When I ask him about the smell of fresh varnish, he smiles and tucks his feet more firmly between the rungs of the stool.

When I consider the myth of the wise woman springing from Zeus's head, two things happen: I fall out of love with Roland Barthes and I begin to think about the man's brain as a womb. It is far worse than when I was little, imagining myself bursting out of my mother's body, examining my own body for possible exit points, knowing it would be excruciating for a baby to get out of me in any way I could imagine.

Danka was married once. *She was pregnant, he says, and we were already sharing an apartment, but it was fine with me. Two days later she disappeared; a week after that she phoned to tell me she had borrowed the money for a New York abortion from the father, and that she wasn't coming back.*

X keeps coming back to speak to me from the doorway of my unbearable room. It is unlike anything I've lived in before: peachy white walls, wicker, flowered cushions, a Dufy print over the couch, one of Danka's paintings of a rioting crowd over the pine table where I work, an ancient cracked yellow bowl of oranges on top of my dresser.

BLACK BRANCH IN YELLOW WIND

That minute when we knew Toby was missing again. Yellow light faltered like warm water, immediately abandoned by my father and his clients, three brothers in heavy white cotton shirts who moved beyond the door, the fence, and into other lives, the elemental quiet, the smell of lavender and polish, and

Those moments are compressed into one recurrent motif—an arm in a black sleeve swings. Yellow light surrounds it like panicky birdsong.

My father is old and lives in a hospital now. He is unable to speak. When I visit him in his room, a nurse brings a tray with yellow pencils and a pad of paper. Holding a pencil in his fist, my father draws a shaky heart, then holds the paper out to me on his open palm, the dry white remains of his tongue.

What has my father done? He left the house while my mother beat me, regularly.

X stands in the doorway and apologizes for coming so late. He has eaten dinner at the Varsity; he still can't cook.

Do you remember the time we overheard that old wino saying that he'd been jailed for twenty years because he shot

his wife? And said he'd do it over again, X says, *given the opportunity?*
No, I tell him. *No, I don't remember that.*

What has X done? He has beaten me regularly.

The wind whispers in the tree outside my bathroom window. A branch scratches at the opaque glass.

I sit in the flowered chair. I have considered forgetting the arm and its downward movement, also considered its later attachment to various exotic strangers and allowing them to walk off into other lives, to take the arm with them as part of themselves: that elegant father-figure walking away, an old wino, a tall, middle-aged woman in a gardening hat, Roland Barthes going to get his motorcycle, a closely imagined god with a woman in his brain who is trying to get out. Purposeful amnesia, however, has its own fingers. It seems likely that with the arm would go both light and movement, which would follow that flesh into other lives.

What do I remember?

My father giving me ice cream in the park. Standing with X beside a couch covered with broken glass. Toby clutching my hand while I ask her what she has done

BLACK BRANCH IN YELLOW WIND

with the soap. A man in a black coat looking straight into my eyes without recognition. Danka walking in sunlight, carrying a naïve portrait of a baby's head.

> *O westron wynde, when wilt thou blow*
> *the small rain down come rain.*
> *Christ that my love were in my arms*
> *and I in my bed again.*
>
> — Anonymous

THE BEAUTIFUL VOICES OF THE MONKS BEHIND THE WALL

For Brother Gerald

◆ Thelma often telephoned once the light was gone. *Let's go somewhere,* she would begin, *come with me.*

I thought I had finished with Thelma when I said goodbye at the door of our rented trailer a year ago. Here, there are long hallways, and snow. I can hear the monks singing. The sound is male and permanent.

The sound white paint makes going on the wall. Gary gets my letter and folds it and puts it in his pocket and keeps painting.

The monks seem to know everything, and so I go on listening. The stinging sound of snow crying because of its whiteness and its purity. The sound of winter coming, if trees had skin.

I tell myself I travelled to the monastery to work, but I have not taken my camera out of its case. I want to photograph what I smell, what I hear. Synesthesia. Wind through pine branches, my forearm exposed, reaching for the pot of butter. The singing of the monks, arctic air burning across the flat land around the flame-red windmill, what it has given up.

The voices are internalized; they rush like water over a dam. Gary's voice, low, sweet, and dishonest, or Thelma's, formidable and swan-like when she was angry, forsythia and smoke when she was telling lies.

Thelma said it was easier to get stoned in Toronto than to drive to Vancouver in the winter, up and down those mountains along the north Superior shore before you reach the flat highway to Winnipeg. I don't know anyone who died of a drug overdose, she told me, dropping a hit of something into her tea, lifting the cup slowly to her lips and sipping at it. When I was nineteen I was certain I'd be dead at twenty-one, Thelma said, and I thought I would live forever. Two heads on the same monster, if you ask me.

Here in the dining room, tiny windows answer with light that cannot reach the cheap flatware marked by endless washing or the rose or the ratty clean oilcloth that covers the table. The light is weak, softened by falling snow.

I don't know the language. I refer to the religious brothers as men, or as monks. These monks are the opposite of sirens when they sing. They are the opposite of men I am used to.

When Thelma mentioned her heart to a man, he did not laugh, he touched her arm. With me she was always harsh; with them, soft as butter and snow. Somewhere inside both of us a smell of lemon juice, the shock of the tongue against the sharp opened top of a can, the taste of tin.

Thelma said it wasn't dangerous for her, only a game to help her concentrate. She did drugs people sold to her, or she sold drugs to them. She said it was against big business, she could be the peasant or the entrepreneur. She photographed a man in convulsions, a girl in a basement washroom on Yonge Street, a girl she'd bought a vial of hash oil from. A photograph was taken after the girl broke a vial on the tile floor and wanted Thelma to pay for it; in the picture the girl's eyes peek through splayed fingers, her hands cover her face. Thelma got a job at a bank, took pictures of women sniffing lines of white powder in the washroom, heads bent over the counter where the mirrors gleamed, looking for the habitual, for a prayer that would always be answered.

The monks and the guests eat their meals at the same time. I rise when they rise, am seated when they sit, but I have never entered the chapel.

I am reaching for the white pot of butter that sits on the yellow oilcloth. The oilcloth has been wiped clean hundreds of times. I am not hungry. There is a rose in a thin aluminum vase and I cannot see well enough to tell whether the rose is real. Every day when I sit down three times at this place to eat, to the freshly wiped oilcloth, I do not try to get closer to the rose, I do not try to see whether the rose is real, whether it wilts and dries, whether it gathers dust in the soft dark folds of its petals.

Thelma lived five days at a time. Her voice racing and thin, she telephoned from Wales and Kauai, from towns in Spain where bulls ran loose in streets crowded with muscular young men, where a goat thrown from a church roof to the cobbled street below in an annual ceremony choked on its own blood. Thelma had her camera; she'd say she took what she saw, as if she had stolen the sight from its place in the world and locked it away.

THE BEAUTIFUL VOICES OF THE MONKS BEHIND THE WALL

My health is bad but the day is beautiful. When I walk out of the guest wing, Brother Derek is shovelling snow that has blown over the sidewalk, his face red up into his thin blond hair with the effort, the sidewalk bare again where he has forced the snow into low piles against the fence. The wind gathers speed over the fields, and when I return the backs of my knees and thighs are red from its whipping.

The flat steel blade turns in the butter, my forearm rests on the slippery oilcloth. I am reading and not reading a letter which has been written to me, which has not been written to me. The windows are small. The light is poor and I cannot see well enough to tell if it is snowing.

Around the corner from Thelma's house people were living in a bus shelter, an old woman and her retarded daughter and a skinny brown cat. Their dog was killed in the fire. In the photographs, the old woman and her daughter crouch against the cold; they have a damp yellow foam mattress and a bag of clothes and a bundle buggy.

I sit with my coffee a long time. My lips move softly against the solid white porcelain when I drink. There is grease on the empty plate in front of me, a bit of potato, a pork chop bone with meat still clinging to it, a dirty plate, a dirty juice glass, dirty fork, knife and spoon, dirty cup.

The voices drift and settle. I remember the butter, I do not remember writing letters to Thelma, receiving her letter. The monks sound different than other men. The skirts of their cassocks brush the floor which has been lovingly wiped clean, the cassocks brush their legs with a sound that is like blackbirds rising from pine branches into the air, and when they raise their arms they make the same sound, cloth against the forearm, thick and soft.

Thelma made statues of the world one way or another, and then she bought a house in it, but it remained like two sides of a mirror and Thelma was on one side and I was on the other. The opposite of time—where I am always in the presence of a moment—in Thelma's continuum I could only pass backward and forward, like Man Ray's painting of the paradoxical stairs, up and down at the same time, but never both at once.

I was hungry when I came downstairs for dinner, when I followed the novice monks down the wrong stairs. I was hungry in my rented room with its cross and its narrow bed and its view of snow and blackbirds.

THE BEAUTIFUL VOICES OF THE MONKS BEHIND THE WALL

At home I play the piano in the dark, that feeling of the cold keys under my fingers. I play very badly. That sound is in the air a little tonight at dinner. The letter is creased where it was folded. I remember meeting Thelma in a restaurant. We were both waiting for other people and could not talk. Her face with its parchment skin. No human voice makes sense at times like these. There is my poor piano sound in the middle of the night that I hope will wake no one, there is a rose that is replaced every day or is made of silk and wire or plastic.

Thelma, drunk, had sliced her hand prying the top off a film canister in the darkroom. She stood in her kitchen, black and white photographs all over the wooden table in front of the vinegar and the crystal salt and pepper shakers. It wasn't a serious cut, I could tell by the way the blood dripped slowly from her palm onto the prints, which were drizzled across with red. I want you to have these, she told me.

I don't have a book about ritual, but the day goes like this: Morning Praise, Community Eucharist, Mid-Day Praise, Vespers, and Vigils.

I hesitate to believe it is snowing; I savour my uncertainty about the solidity of the wall between me and the monks' dining room. I have never seen the monks' dining room, but I believe in that room, even though I only imagine it. I am certain it takes up space because I have been in the hallways around it, and have seen the door that leads to it from the kitchen.

Come on, come with me. A cheap flight to somewhere warm and crazy.

Snow deforms the visual spikes of the landscape and unifies everything, simplifies, buries colour. White rejects the spectrum, black absorbs colour and heats up with every shade of light.

When my food is in front of me, I eat. When my dinner plate is piled with shredded lettuce, a fried pork chop, hot and greasy, pickled beets, and grey boiled potatoes, I eat.

Thelma came to see me; she had stolen some bread. Plastic bread packages dangled from both hands. She stood in the rain on my porch with her coat undone.

Everything has dissolved in the soup. Cabbage and celery boiled with pork bones, water, and salt, until released from form. The long strips are the colour of lake water in a bowl. I wind them on my spoon and carry them to my mouth.

Often at night I hear them outside my door. A monk is assigned to patrol the guest wing. The monks are old-fashioned. They wear rope belts and the skirts of their cassocks brush the tops of their feet. Often they pass in twos and I hear them whispering.

I do not want to sleep or eat but these things are available and pleasant. So much is done because it is available and pleasant.

Thelma went out that afternoon to steal bread because the man next door was bleeding from the ears and wouldn't go with her to the hospital. Speed. His girlfriend believed there were people outside the windows shining mirrors in at her. Maybe there were. She ran from room to room, but the people with the mirrors beat her to every window. The lake gleamed at the end of the street.

When I received the letter I folded it again and again until it was small as a cube of sugar. The paper bears those creases, the typewritten letters are broken. *Which is more difficult for you*, the letter asks in one place, *to live alone and go from man to man, or to live the* semi-ascetic life of marriage? Whichever is the more difficult path is the one you should follow.

I hate the word *follow*.

Among the photographs on Thelma's kitchen table: a man peeing into a beer glass in the super's basement apartment. The skin of a man's back, endless and pale as the Canadian flatlands under snow. A statue surrounded by pine trees and smoke.

Burning golden liquid in the throat, song or liquor, yes, I could force down one more mouthful, Thelma across the table from me gleaming with it, black lashes wet from laughing. We told each other lies and we didn't care, what each of us once wanted was gone forever and this was all we knew, sitting at the table of a rented trailer perched on a precipice in the middle of nowhere. Sunlight laboured across the plastic tablecloth until finally the purple twilight was kind enough to remain outside the window. *My mother was a jazz singer in Arizona*, Thelma said. *My father was a waiter in Montreal*, I answered. *A toast to the mind parasites*, said Thelma, drinking from a peanut butter jar topped up with lemon gin, *a toast to brave Chilean flautists and the makers of painted wooden lawn ornaments.*

THE BEAUTIFUL VOICES OF THE MONKS BEHIND THE WALL

In the envelope with the letter there were several black and white portraits: Phil Ochs, Gwendolyn MacEwen, Diane Arbus, Sylvia Plath, Thelma. In moments of despair I admit that I will never touch the polished ancient wood of the monks' table. I have imagined linen and silver, tall candles so thick they stand on the table without support.

Only those who have never known evil do not feel an impelling need for goodness. And even then, I go on, writing a letter mentally, if it was long ago they will forget, just as pain is forgotten, and a long white scar becomes the abstract hieroglyph of an experience that can now be repeated. Hand the scissors, hand the scissors by the blades.

I've made a list of all the men I could remember who'd asked me to bed. I included only those who had been forthright. There were more men on the list than there are monks here, but I thought of those men affectionately, as if suddenly seeing them in a group, when I followed the novice monks down the wrong stairs.

I went with Thelma to steal bread from the skids outside the IGA at three in the morning. White bread. Stolen steaks tucked in the stroller behind the baby. The trucker in the apartment downstairs from Thelma's was beating his wife again. She stood in the backyard in her nightgown, screaming, but the police came because the country music was so loud. Watching from an upstairs window Thelma ducked down, listening to Phyllis Schlafly or to Germany on the short wave. It was a noisy night but Thelma's pictures of it were serene and silent. The nightgown was pink and nylon, the woman's feet bare in the damp grass.

Once someone has been dead long enough you can legally steal their words. Photographs make it possible to stare and stare into the eyes of strangers, as once you could stare only at the dead.

Watch Thelma, ecstatic, with her camera in the middle of a storm, the grey sky boiling with dark cloud over the peaked roofs on her street, the hem of her cotton raincoat dripping on her legs and shoes, her feet splashing through puddles, the wet skin of her face running with water and shining, impermeable as porcelain.

I want tight black silk or a blueberry branch and lichen on rock. I have the hideous banality of repetition, sleep that comes from numbers, the treachery of stairs and roses. Do the monks take turns at penitence, or do they kneel together in the chapel and offer their transgressions to a perfect glaring image on the altar? To ask a question is to want, I add to my letter, to imagine is to know.

Thelma had a room I didn't know about. The day she dripped blood on the pictures, she left a door ajar that I'd always thought led to a closet. What I saw on the walls behind her was unmitigated by art: unfocused ruins, blood, and the blurred dead faces of children.

There is a bend in the snow-covered road that leads to the hamlet of Pewter. The parish cathedral was beautifully painted with murals by a monk in the nineteenth century, and when the monks travel (and they do, in their newsletter there are photographs of some of them in other monasteries, at conventions, barbecuing, conducting classes) they return with gifts to decorate the church. This has become something of a pleasant contest. I would like to walk to the cathedral but it is over four miles, and forty below zero. As it is, the woman at the cash register in the café warns me to wrap up. *Half a mile is a long way in that wicked cold,* she says, turning to pour coffee. The people at the café are used to visitors walking down from the monastery, they watch me unwrap my long grey scarf stiffened with ice, not so many guests in the winter, not many walk down through the snow. *Don't even try going to the cathedral, the kind woman warns, you wouldn't make it past the hill.*

Come on, let's go. We'll burn up Peru. Come with me.

The idea of the trailer was that we were going to help each other get clean. At six o'clock in the morning we finished the last of the Jack Daniel's and Thelma suggested we go swimming. Wisps of white mist hung over the black water that lay still as a mirror. We undressed in the tiny kitchen, nearly falling more than once, and shook ourselves like runners as we passed under the awning. I had never seen Thelma naked, and couldn't help glancing at her loosening thighs and pendulous brown-tipped breasts as we marched like martinets across grass, gravel, and the sand where we'd stumbled hunting for turtle eggs. We stepped into the lake without slowing down, as if we'd never been immersed in water before. The water was very cold, and though the soles of our feet ached on large sharp stones, neither of us cried out or laughed. Thelma swam ahead quickly, toward the small island haunted by harmless black water snakes, and did not seem to mind splashing wildly and then gargling so that the lake echoed with her voice and thrashing. She turned on her back and waved to me, laughing and shrieking. She was enjoying herself breaking the silence. At that time, she was still trying to communicate. *Come on,* she yelled, and howled like a loon. *Come on, come on.*

Three sets of tracks, a yellow grain elevator, a grocery co-op, and a hotel the colour of geraniums. Red here is hot, burns the eye next to the burning white of the snow. The topic daily at the café, among the women, is the deformed baby of one of their daughters.

The hotel doors have black handles. At the co-op, selecting apples for my nightly snack, I try to convince myself that I could go into the bar and have a look around. A single glass of Scotch. Then write the letter. Too cold to take the Rollei out, too intrusive at the monastery, I can't work as I'd intended.

Don't be afraid. Come with me. Come on, what's the matter? Out of here, cheap and crazy.

I watched Thelma hungrily sip at the last of the Scotch. The tackiness of the trailer was getting to me, the flowered curtains, the orange and blue wallpaper, the green shag rug. I took the camera out, aimed at the floor, at Thelma's mouth, moved closer to her, close enough to burn the slurp of lip and liquid onto film.

Caught Thelma's surprise. Thelma put the glass down on the brown table, shoved it across at me. *I need this stuff*, she said, *I don't have your simple husband to fall back on in the dead of night. You*, she said, squinting at me, *you haven't been able to stand up straight for weeks. You think you're here to save me*, said Thelma, *but I'm giving you permission. You're in with me up to your neck. Let's phone Gary and tell him we're flying to the Côte d'Azur.* I grabbed the receiver from her hand and yanked the wire out of the wall. The next morning I walked into town and phoned him myself, told him I was ready to go home.

We told each other lies and Thelma didn't care. Thelma made herself up as she went along, out of good times and compliments. I kept believing there was more to her, even when she got drunk and told me I was letting my life drain away. *You and I could be having a hot time in Brazil*, said Thelma, dumping the last of the Scotch into her own glass and belting it back, *we could be fucking seventeen-year-olds and taking arty pictures of them afterwards instead of pining away up here.* I listened to her intently. I was listening for Thelma's voice to clarify, the way you wait for leaves to settle in Chinese tea. But Thelma's voice went on, hard and raucous, she was describing what she'd do with her young man, and I listened and imagined in spite of myself how I would photograph the room, the skin and bed, if I were there. I wanted to be alone but the trailer was small. Something was hidden in Thelma that I wanted to see, that I needed. I had to go on listening.

When Thelma worked, she was intense and admirable. We were sitting in the darkroom while Thelma cut hundred-foot rolls of film down to fit in canisters. Her voice came mixed with the smell of developer and the turning sound of the little mechanical handle. *Me, I'm loyal; I'd chop my arm off for you,* said Thelma. I said, *You remember that woman in the Carson McCullers story, the one who cut off her own nipples at the end, that's the thing, that deformity for a gesture, what you're talking about is pure gesture.* Yes, said Thelma, *but the operative word there, something you'll never understand, is not gesture, but purity.*

The letter arrived several days after Thelma's death. They said she set the fire herself. The letter bore no salutation, no signature. It contained questions and an invitation to join her. I stay in the monastery and work on my reply.

Dinner is over and the guests can line up for coffee. The cups are thick old porcelain that has been wiped clean a thousand times. Soft lips do no damage, soft lips on china all around me.

Every day language becomes more inexact; soft pads at the ends of fingers press piano keys. The yellow oilcloth has been wiped clean again; air moves around a rose that is replaced or is made of silk and wire or plastic. The coffee is perfect today. The precision of harmony.

The novices, men who have not yet been accepted into the order, are not allowed skirts. They wear sports coats and trousers and they appear very ordinary and worried. One evening after Vespers I took a wrong turn and followed the novices down their stairs, the stairs of the monks going to dinner, and they turned and shushed and motioned to me. The monks eat sequestered together in their own room. I have been told they eat in silence.

BIG OZ

MORNING

◆ The heart-shaped ashtray is made of onyx, a semi-translucent stone. Full of ashes and burnt matches, it sits in the middle of the table, gathering and expelling light. Beside the ashtray are a deck of worn red playing cards, beer bottles in various states of emptiness, a packet of cigarette papers, and a white french fries box streaked with gravy. There is a map of Ontario, sliced into triangular bits by an X-acto knife which still lies beside the multi-coloured pieces; the knife blade points toward the only window in the room.

The table is made of particle board, and so low it must be knelt at. To one side, there is a long plaid chesterfield with the seat cushions removed; to the other, two large armchairs of the square sort often found in cottages. She sits on the floor with her elbows on the low table. On the chairs, and on the chesterfield, and on the cushions which have been removed from the chesterfield and placed in a line on the floor near the window, there are shadows which, when moving, will become people again.

She can't sleep. She lifts one of the beer bottles and

sips at what is warm and remaining in it. It tastes bad but wet. She empties all of the bottles. One shadow snores; another speaks gibberish out of a dream. The room is dark except for yellow light shining through the half-open bathroom door, and the tentative dawn that she knows would be vivid blue at the far side of the lake if she bothered to rouse herself and look.

Red light flares against the living-room wall, garishly illuminating the plaid back of the chesterfield, a cheap Emily Carr print, and fabric lampshades. She stands, brushing the knees of her pants with quick slaps, her legs stiff from kneeling. Outside, on the shale below the cedar deck, an Ontario Provincial Police car has parked. The police can be coming only here; the cottage sits alone on this part of the bay, some executive's idea of a country hideaway. She slips the cigarette papers into her pocket, stoops to grab the bag of dope off the floor beside her, and by instinct or habit has the toilet flushed before the police can even knock. She is glad she is awake, as if this gives a purpose to her insomnia, and she opens the front door without waking anyone.

The sky is lit with orange behind their blue shoulders, streaks of orange and white clouds cut with black birds. They are both wearing full uniforms, and their guns are visible. The nearer one stands stiffly. The other leans on the rail as if waiting, but he speaks first:

BIG OZ

Whose cottage is this?

I don't know, she says, *a friend of a friend ...*

Your name please?

She tells him.

Who else is here?

The nearer one is writing everything down in a small leatherbound steno book. She can smell garlic, aftershave. She is really drunk, drunker than she thought when she was sitting silent in the dark. She savours every attempt to form a word.

She tells him. *They're all asleep.*

Party here last night? asks the first officer, the one with the book.

Yes, she says, *what is this about?*

Lot of people out, would you say?

Yes.

Notice a woman with long brown hair in a blue shirt and white skirt?

She thinks for a moment.

Maybe carrying a thin Chinese bedroll?

I don't know, she says, trying to remember. She feels them at her back then, three or four of the others, awake, crowding around the doorway in sleepy silence. I don't know, she says. Why? What happened?

The officer on the rail says, A woman was found dead this morning on the beach. It's possible she was murdered, but maybe she was just so stoned she rolled into the water in her sleep.

MORNING

Wearing matching pink cotton bathing-suits smocked across the chest, the two sisters sit side by side on chrome chairs at the kitchen table. Thin straps dig into their shoulders, and one of the girls plucks with her fingers at the folded towels piled in front of her while she waits. The sisters can see their mother on the chesterfield with Harry in the living room. There is danceable

BIG OZ

jazz playing on the hi-fi; the dusty air goes around in the sun coming in the window. Harry has a little red car made of steel with tiny glass windows and no driver, and he is running the little car down their mother's arm and back up it again. He spins the rubber wheels with his thumb, then runs the car along and along her leg.

MORNING

Jan isn't crying, but his eyes are wide open and his hands are cupped around his cheeks as if he is trying not to. He has eaten the cucumber sandwich the waitress put in front of him, but mechanically, politely, decades of civility in no way touched by his present distress. His shirt is clean, pressed, starched, perfect, his copper-rimmed glasses shine. For a moment she thinks she knows what draws him to the woman he is speaking about.

And after they left? she asks sadly, happy she was fortified by smooth hot lungfuls of golden hash in the car before she came in to meet him.

She just walked out again, he says.

She can see all the white of a hospital lobby when she looks at his shirt, at the sapphire glinting on his tie-clip.

MORNING

She focuses with difficulty on the lights ahead of her. Bright, rectangular and red, the lights stare out from holes stamped in the white metal body of the other car. Breathing slowly, she flexes her stiff fingers on the steering wheel, alert inside a new wave of dizziness. His hand, still half-tangled in silk up under her skirt, has stopped, and cold air travels along her thighs to a point where his wrist is keeping her skin deliciously warm.

The highway is twelve lanes wide here, yellow-grey concrete slick under light fog, split by metal rails and pilons and great white overpasses where headlights curve. She is familiar with the road, but not where she's going. The plan had been to drive somewhere. He is supposed to give her directions, but he is unconscious, his head back against the blue seat, his mouth open, eyes closed. She's tens of kilometres over the speed limit, but she wants to stay within reach of the comfort of the lights of the Mercedes ahead of her. The sky above is heavy with black cloud. She is careful as she lets go of the wheel with one hand to turn up the heater.

It is at this moment that she hits the yellow curb with the wheels on the left side of the car. There is a

BIG OZ

clunk of metal on stone, the steering wheel jerks in her hand, a white wall rises in her vision to the left, and she veers back onto the road, over-correcting until she slows. He hasn't even woken up. The same sound is repeated and repeated, but she is in the fast lane where she meant to be, she isn't driving into anything. And then she sees it in the rear-view mirror, a hubcap rolling away, spinning like a toy, and she laughs and laughs.

MORNING

She's always been curious about the effects on other people. She just waits for it to be over, the buzz, the high, the giddiness, at least once the most intense effects have worn off. She watches Jan. One beer after another, the way he moves his mouth around the bottle, then his cigarette, then around whatever is being passed from hand to hand, his arm bending up toward his face, the way he smiles, sitting up a little straighter, when she makes a joke. He is intense then, intense and a bit sloppy, how can it be entertaining to make your body stumble in familiar hallways, to drop your fork full of pasta on the floor in a restaurant, to make navigating a zipper seem like advanced calculus? Then to drag that expensively induced smeared and fumbling vision home and into a false and lonely sleep. Yet she does this, anticipates it, day after day.

MORNING

She's still at Jan's at three in the morning, playing hearts with Sarah and Francis, when they hear August singing at the top of the stairs. The house is laid out so that when you are at the dining-room table, a large wooden oblong with great thick legs, you are doused in yellow light from a massive antique chandelier they bought at auction and which hangs, brassy and golden, from the centre of the ceiling. They put their cards face down and turn to watch August, who seems to be attempting the last aria from *Aida* in a strained falsetto. He is dressed in a long satin kimono which looks ridiculous with his thinning bronze hair and hairy calves. August's tenuous hold on dignity is lost when he puts one hand to his chest and the other sweeps before him in a gesture of magnanimity, throwing him off-balance. He falls on his back, slides, bumping, down the soft carpeted surface of the stairs before any of them can move. He comes to a stop with his feet against the umbrella stand, his head a few steps above. *Nothing broken, I don't think,* August says to them calmly, but they all get up to find their coats.

AFTERNOON

Uncle Ned says they figured the old guy was bashing her around because they drank so much, more bottles than food when they filled the back seat of the car with supplies on Saturday, both of them on pension and sort of isolated in that place way out on the highway. So what if he'd been Justice of the Peace in town for thirty years? *Later though, when they discovered that he'd had a brain tumour, and that that was what had killed him,* Uncle Ned says, *I was pretty relieved.*

AFTERNOON

Jan circles the table, legs flexed like a skier's so that his eyes are on the same level as the silverware. *Look at the colour,* he says, *would you like a glass?* She would. The bottle has been uncorked for an hour, and he pours for himself, watching the liquid drain slowly down, as if it was a hand sliding up between his thighs.

AFTERNOON

Andy says to her, *That girl could have stolen your skirt and blouse. It might be your clothes she was wearing when she drowned. Or maybe somebody thought it was you and killed* her, eh? *Seeing her hair and your clothes on her maybe somebody just wanted you dead that minute, and rolled her in, thinking she was you sleeping.* Somebody tells Andy to shut up and not be crazy.

You'll find out it was her clothes that dead woman was wearing, Andy insists, leaning back in his chair and squinting and then playing a ten of hearts, hard, so it slides across the table and onto the floor. *Never mind,* somebody says to him, *I know that trick, just sit, I'll get the fucking card for you.*

The cops were supposed to be back here by now, somebody else says, *I've got things to do at home. Are we supposed to hang around here all weekend?*

There might be an inquest.

She sits on a cushioned bench by the window and looks at the water, smooth and stupid, hair in it, how long hair gets caught around your arms when you try to move in water, curled and sticking to the skin; wet, it is strong as rope. How the shock of cold must have been too late to sober her up; under water, you get dizzy, not knowing which way is up, and in the dark, too, once it is all around you, air doesn't feel any different from the cool water pulling you down with your soaking clothes after you roll into a nightmare. Maybe the booze put her farther under what was normally there, or maybe that woman just reached her arms out—she sits thinking as she looks out the window at the water—reached out with everything, her mouth open to take it all in, and found something, anything, there, and wanted it.

EVENING

It's Hallowe'en and they get in and out of cars going from party to party, wherever one is, this one at a television station that's dull, this one at a club on Queen Street West where a man with no expression on his face is singing loudly on stage and another man dressed in a giant bee outfit is dancing, his gossamer wings rimmed with silver sequins. Somewhere else the doors are open to the street and people are screaming. They are having a contest. After they get out of the cab, one of the women with them, with a heavily made-up face and dyed black hair, stops and says, *I've lost my necklace, I've lost it, this can't be*, and they get lucky and hail the cab back and search it, but the necklace is gone and the woman talks of nothing else for the next hour, until at a gallery opening a man in a black cape turns dramatically and spills a large glass of red wine, splashing all of them.

EVENING

She gets him on the ground somehow, maybe a story

about worms does it. She loves him. Looking at his hands in the dim light, at his smooth chin, the delicate collarbone inside his open collar, she strokes his thigh and turns his face to look at her. Her own shirt is half-open; she leans forward to kiss his neck. The smell of grass, of beer, of clean clothing near him. There's no one else around, it's dark, she wants him here and he knows it. But he stands up spanking his jeans to get the grass off—spiders, bits of dry leaves, memories, she imagines. This time he just isn't drunk enough.

EVENING

He doesn't like it when she's thinking gothic, artificially destroying what little equilibrium she has. A story about a woman whose hands were cut off after she was raped, a story about a woman abandoning her baby in the cold. His hands are shaking, his face unshaven. His skin is an off-yellow colour it would normally be only if he was ill. *What in god's name*, she thinks, *are we doing in Montreal?*

EVENING

She and her sister read the magazines that are stuck haphazardly into the brass stand topped with an ashtray full of unfiltered cigarette butts. CAR-toon, Hotdogger. They don't like these magazines, which belong to one of their uncles; they read bits to each other every now and then in sarcastic voices, reach out to adjust a lampshade, stare at the floor, have another cookie and a sip of warm milk. There's nothing else to do. Their two aunts, Beryl and Ginny, and their mother, are in the kitchen, drinking. After a while, the women will laugh more loudly, and after that, they will argue. The sisters will fall asleep on the chairs in their clothes; they will wake up, stiff and sweaty, under coats someone has thrown over them during the night, coats smelling of people they don't know.

EVENING

She goes into the bar looking for Sunny, who said he'd have something by eight o'clock. It's nine now, she knows he's always here, and he is, wearing a black T-shirt and sitting at a long table with several men and women who look like bikers. He gets up and nods and when she sits beside him he tells her the other guy hasn't come yet, the connection, so she might as well have a beer, and he pours her one out of a large jug, into a glass that's already been used. The conversation rages like a wave up and down the table, some kind of contest ensuing, during which most of them get up, stand at one end of the table, slide down their zippers, and use a pencil borrowed from the waiter. Sunny is middling on this deal; she wonders how this is going to work, her giving Sunny the money and then getting the dope from the guy who's late. Maybe he isn't coming. This happens a lot. Sunny is telling her the story of his life again and staring at her legs. But the guy does show up; she gives the money to Sunny, watches him pocket the difference between what he told her and what the guy told him, and then he tells her she might as well finish her drink, which he tops up from the warm draught in the pitcher. She's sitting there with a pound of dope on her lap in a brown paper bag when a policeman walks into the bar, followed by another cop with a haughty look. She sits still. No one cares what happens now, she paid for the drugs, these people are not her friends. Half of them are aware of what went down, and all of them are drunk. The first cop comes over, but to the wrong end of the table, and she drinks her beer, sipping at it silently, trying not to move too suddenly, trying not to look any more worried than she ought to be in this bar. The cops leave, nodding to the table; and a guy, maybe the guy who had the biggest penis in the contest, says, *They were after Snake. He sliced some guy up downtown.* And then she leaves.

BIG OZ

EVENING

She abandons the scent of Gitanes and cheap draught and the tightly packed padded chairs and the loud blues music and swings past the payphone on the wall and says goodbye to the manager who is standing behind a till near the door and comes out into cold air that seems to lick her face. Her hands tingle, and her feet, crammed into tight leather shoes, want to dance. For a mile up Spadina she kisses every tree she sees, the small struggling ones held up by black wrought-iron cages and the sturdy thick ones beside the Wing On Funeral Home farther north. To a couple passing by she sings, *Forget every trouble*. Returning to a tree, which one, one that has already been kissed, she doesn't remember, but she tells it what she thinks, *Thank god*.

MORNING

Examining his university-teacher clothing strewn over the floor, and the books stacked in teetering piles, their dinner dishes from the night before, wine glasses, and a bowl with a few popcorn kernels left in the bottom, from her perch on the side of the bed, she says, *I think I know why we do this. It's because of a desire to live in the perpetual present.*

She spoils it for him this way, she knows, but she doesn't care in the least. She watches for one of his typical reactions: the return of lust to the eyes, a fidgety movement toward watch and pants, a comment on the weather. He says, *What is?*

As if you were an errand girl with a mesh bag and a shopping list in your own life, she says, *as if you were only a clerk in the dream.*

She stands up, thinking of that woman sneaking into the back bedroom of the cottage, stealing her white skirt and blue blouse, stumbling through the crowded living room and out to the cold fresh air of the beach, hearing the water and its soothing tug on the land in the dark, smelling pine and cedar and seaweed, spreading the cotton bedroll out on the sand.

She's got a clipping here somewhere. *Woman Found Dead on Beach.* She should find it and show it to him.

He is already sitting up in bed with a large book on his lap. Spread out on top of the book are the cigarette papers and the little plastic bag, the matches with a few rectangular pieces missing from the cover that he used for makeshift filters in the joints he rolled.

She picks up a clay ashtray her daughter made when she was little, and throws it at the grey light coming through the window. Against the glass, the ashtray disintegrates into small pink pieces that spray back into the room as if thrown from outside. The window bells slightly but remains intact. He is silent, his lips forming an 'oh' around the joint.

She says, *Because of fear, then.*

She says this to him because she wants him to hear it, thinks maybe they could both believe it was that simple. The way two or three times a year she makes a list that includes things like: *go swimming every wednesday, buy white skirt, research vitamins, quit smoking.* But she is feeling the warmth of a bedroll on sand, the way the darkness leans in, how every soft moment has been concentrated in the slow touch of shore water on skin. She is taken by an ornate dizziness more complicated than anything induced by spinning, the kind of vertigo that makes you hear things: like a low voice, maybe his, maybe hers, saying, *It's warmer in bed, we can clean up the mess later.*

HIS DOGS

◆ Esorr Yvales takes his gun and his dogs to a certain part of the backyard under the lilac tree. Esorr examines his dogs. With their cropped ears and tails, the three of them look particularly vicious. Fourier shivers and noses the blossoms trailing over her back. The tree is in full bloom. Esorr fingers the barrel of the .22 calibre automatic pistol in his pocket, and stares.

His dogs have long legs, narrow heads, and eyes which move up and down sideways. They are classics of their breed. The three of them glare back at him without interest. Murder is not out of the question at this moment; the dogs turning on Esorr, Esorr lifting the pistol to shoot them, one at a time.

The smell of flowers numbs them, and the moment passes. The attention of the dogs has shifted, from Esorr and the sound of the metal barrel inside his nylon jacket pocket, to a brown squirrel edging from a white railing onto his neighbour's Chinese elm. Esorr's heart, which was firm and resolved, softens into love. His dogs, his gun, his backyard. Narcosis, sentiment, narcissism. The power to kill his dogs remains with him, and allows him to love his dogs all the more.

Why should things fall down? asks Esorr, *why should things fall down?*

◆

What is beautiful in Esorr's world? Well, the three dogs, for one thing. Disobedient, glossy flanked, and reticent: Ignatius, Fourier, and Justine.

Out of the corner of his eye, Esorr's dogs resemble smudges of smoke against the sky, if the sky were green; or the ghosts of small horses; or shapes from Braque's *The Chair* in motion.

Things against his skin. Esorr stands for a moment, lost between irritation at so many impingements on his thinking and the perfect blending of fabric at every fold of his body: the thick cotton of his shorts hugging his groin, the nylon of his jacket rubbing his armpits, the cool worsted of his tailored trousers sluiced against the backs of his knees at each terrible step. At each terrible step he moves farther away from his dogs and his love of them, and closer to a desire to go back and shoot them, one by one.

Am I trying to forget what they did? Esorr begs himself, *am I trying to forget what they did?*

HIS DOGS

◆

His dogs appear ancient and noble. They command respect with their bearing and their presence. Ignatius has been to church; Fourier to the university grounds; and Justine has been allowed to sleep in Esorr's bedroom. One of the reasons, one of the secondary reasons, that Esorr believes he will have to shoot them, is that they know more than he does. They are wise. Their look, when they deign to look at him, alternates between condescension and dismissal, humility and sacrilege, omniscience and blindness.

The three dogs walk in a group with a similar gait; only Esorr can tell them apart. There are three of them, and three is a sacred number in Esorr's eyes. This is the kind of reason Esorr gives himself for wanting to kill his dogs: there should not be a sacred number of dogs. The thought that the dogs are of a sacred number should never occur to him, he thinks; nor should the idea that he might need to shoot some dogs because he is afraid of having a sacred idea about how many of them he has.

Esorr's dogs are hundreds of years old and this causes him anxiety. When he allows Ignatius to be exercised by the neighbourly widow, the one with the orange kiss-curls, whom he admires for her ability to fill the air with the scent of chicken and muffins, he is afraid she will notice something and cross-examine him on her return. And then after, Esorr can't help thinking—after he has provided her with unsatisfactory answers—after, she will tell others that his dogs are ancient and sacred. Somehow, he fears, her knowing and the blithe dissemination of that information will make it impossible for him to shoot his dogs in private. Someone will demand an investigation or a ceremony.

Comme d'habitude? Esorr implores himself, *comme d'habitude?*

◆

His dogs have saved babies drowning in the sea, and alerted an elderly couple to a fire in their kitchen. His dogs have wandered through marsh and wetlands between the hunters and the herons. His dogs have danced in a certain formation and halted rioters at the point of descent into chaos.

Esorr has seen his dogs hold dripping raw liver in their mouths; he has seen them sniff piles of excrement joyfully, and lick up vomit; he has seen them roll in the mess of a long-dead rabbit carcass and later urinate on trees and on the back wheels of blue Studebakers; he has watched them defecate on concrete, broken glass, and pristine lawns.

HIS DOGS

Dogrose, dog's tooth violets, dogstones, dog's-tongue, dogbane, and doggrass grow in carefully tended patches in his backyard. Dogbane is rumoured to be poisonous to dogs when ingested by them. Esorr examines a leaf from the dogbane plant by holding it up to the light and tries to see his dogs through it. No contest, Esorr determines. The invisibility of his dogs through the leaf that would poison them is complete. The impassivity of the poisonous leaf to the light carrying the image of his dogs is total.

Is the gun hungry? Esorr explores himself for an explanation, *is the gun hungry, so that it has nothing to do with me at all?*

◆

Sacred dogs. Hallelujah dogs. Gris-gris dogs to set free and follow through the town, determining the future with their meanderings. This dog goes to this building, where Esorr will find employment. This dog befriends this woman, whom Esorr will marry. This dog sniffs a casement window of the lodging house, where Esorr will discover a perfectly square room and a congenial atmosphere.

Esorr strokes his gun with his right hand. I am trying to forget the previous owners, he thinks. I am trying to cultivate the transparent organism which will allow me to poison the dogs and see them at the same time.

Euphonious dogs. Choral dogs. Dogs to set humming with the promise of a banquet of dead chickens. Ancient dogs who sing together in moonlight, their throats immaculately stretched up, mouths opened shamelessly in a barely discernible harmony of second tones. Dogs who have lived so long they are patient and create music in gentle undulations of the tongue and throat; his are old dogs who are almost the same dog, they have been so much together.

Will someone come for the dogs? Esorr demands of himself, groping for the squirrel inside the Chinese elm with his left hand, *will someone come for the dogs?*

◆

Esorr's dogs exist and they do not exist. When he walks behind them through the streets, employing the covered shovel, or when he must tug savagely on the leash as they surge toward another dog in primitive jealousy, he feels the awful pressure of possessing them.

When Esorr sleeps, his dogs become invisible to him. Occasionally, they speak to him in the night, their voices theophanous and urgent, reminding him of gun and lilac and love. They chew at his dreams, and the

HIS DOGS

sound of dogs gulping swallows his thinking and his flesh and wakes him in a sweaty panic.

Esorr knows that if he goes away and forgets his dogs they will be destroyed. He knows that if he travels far away, and leaves the dogs behind, three ideas will remain with him forever, even after the dogs have ceased to exist.

Nothing to impede my progress? Esorr asks, *nothing to impede my progress?*

◆

Machine dogs are what Esorr sees when he stares at his dogs from a certain portion of the backyard under the lilac tree. Moving in that oiled way, opening their mouths with the precision of small muscled backhoes over the dead chickens, their nails click metallic on the patio stones as they hover forward and backward over their evening meal.

Esorr snaps off a dogbane leaf and stares into it. He throws the leaf at his monster-truck dogs, his assembly line of chicken-eating dogs, his dogs that smell of carbon monoxide and stare at him with planned, ovate eyes.

Invariably, they finish their meal without incident. Invariably, the moment of panic—when Esorr realizes that gun and dogs are related in a precise and irremediable way, when he begins to believe that he will be unable to shoot his dogs in private because someone will demand an investigation or a ceremony, when he determines that the gun and the dogs both will attack him if he allows them to communicate—at that moment the smell of flowers numbs him, and the moment passes, and he loves them, his dogs, his dogs, his dogs.

EIGHT SCENES:
SOME TANGLED, SOME PLAIN

O N E

◆ You live a couple of miles from here and have never seen a train go by, but it is still unnerving to be tied to the tracks. She has used long scarves, and lengths of lace, and thin nylon ribbon. Her fingers are small, but strong and nimble; the knots she made were learned and practised; it will take her several minutes to untie you. The iron of the tracks is black and rusted, the ties are grey and dry, and there is a white gravel bed underneath. Your knees are slung over the bottom rail, and the back of your neck rests on the other, your head uncomfortably hanging down the metal ridge. The two of you are equally committed to what you are doing, however, and you do not complain. There are bits of grass in your hair, dust on your arm and on your yellow gingham skirt and black shoes. The sun is pleasantly warm as the knots come undone. A mild breeze pushes at the shrubs and small trees that line the right of way, where you keep watch for wild dogs. The grass has not been cut for a long time, and dried and dusty weeds catch in her skirt as she works at the lace knotted around your waist. At this point, something is over. There is no entertainment in undoing what you have done so far. When you are finally sitting up, your friend says, *All right, then, it's my turn*, and you trade places. You shake your skirt and flip your hair to get the dirt out of it, then slowly begin to tie her to the tracks, winding lengths of rag and lace under the ties where the earth allows it, and around the rails under her knees and around her neck.

You have done this before. Trailing around the house, gathering materials, different every week, you ignore chains and electrical wire and extension cords for the softer items you like to feel around your knees and waists: a blue chambray rag, a cashmere scarf with soft fringes, a strip of fine yellow wool.

You hear the train at the same time. It is coming from the same direction as the wind, rumbling, and at first that's what you think it is, but the wind doesn't send ahead the smell of oily dust. Neither of you starts. You begin untying knots as rapidly as you can. Your hands do not shake. You take all advantage of your strong fingernails, and manage to tear the wool holding one of her legs to the iron. Gravel drives into your ankles and dry wood slivers press against your hip as you lean forward to untie your friend's neck. The train is

EIGHT SCENES: SOME TANGLED, SOME PLAIN

visible, an approaching height, not terror yet. You work your fingers to free your friend's wrists. This makes sense. With her hands free she will be able to undo knots as well. With her hands free, she may be able to force herself out of her supine position and walk away.

But she does not. She takes her free hands and grips you about the neck, tightly. She brings your face down to her chest. She is wasting time. You wriggle, force your knees hard into the dirt, against the rail, and pull back. Fingernails dig into the soft skin of your shoulders, and you are surprised to see your friend's calm face looking up at the sky as the train noise becomes real and present and the rush of its air can be felt on your skin. You work stupidly at the knots, you take your teeth down to the cloth and wrench her other knee free, you bite through the lace at her waist and rip that, too, feeling blood on your chin. The train is coming but she stays lying on the tracks looking up at the sky with a patient face. You slide backward down the embankment, you pull on her feet as the train slides by and leaves you holding something partial. The weeds move like the wind moves weeds, and you expect, touching her warm ankle with your fingers, you expect the ground to be shuddering, but it is not, because underneath it is knotted and knotted and knotted to itself, to the weeds, to the train.

TWO

You have never had any facility with marionettes but your Auntie Ida certainly does. Auntie Ida travels around the world. Inevitably, when she comes back, she brings another puppet for you.

The puppets hang in your room. By the time you are six, there are several of them on the wall, the hooks spaced out so that wooden or plastic shoes do not touch woollen or enamelled hair. Auntie Ida can work two marionettes at once: the little Dutch girl with her white cotton hat and blue dress along with the little ballerina with her coiffed hair and pink tutu. Auntie Ida holds one cross-piece in each hand, and tugs the strings adeptly with her fingers while her mouth nearly keeps still and seems not to be speaking at all. You lie on the floor with your chin in your hands near the corner of the bed, while the marionettes walk in mid-air under the bedskirt, which has been pulled up for the occasion, something like a curtain. Auntie Ida has plans to build a puppet theatre some time, a real wooden one that hides you.

The stories Auntie Ida makes the puppets speak are always the same, you think; the puppets are always learning something about themselves. You like the one that goes *pretty is as pretty does*, about the girl who is

EIGHT SCENES: SOME TANGLED, SOME PLAIN

beautiful but cruel and stupid, and the girl who is plain but warm and honest. You like *the girl who cried wolf*, about the girl who was always lying, and then when there was a real wolf, no one believed her. The puppets tell stories, and stories have people in them that things happen to.

THREE

You are sitting in a green metal chair. To your left, there are windows. None of the windows are open. In front of you is a large rectangle of white paper nearly covering the flat plastic surface of a desk that has been pushed together with seven other desks. Old juice tins filled with paint sit where the desks meet. Brush handles stick out of the tins. The girl sitting across from you is squinting at her paper. The girl sitting to your right has already made a tree. The tree has a brown trunk with drips leading up to it, a round green ball for a top, and reddish spots that are supposed to be apples turning brown in the green paint. The teacher said to paint the sky. You ask the girl across from you how to do the sun. She shrugs. To the right of her treetop, the other girl has made a yellow circle with thick yellow bars emanating from it. This is a sun, and you paint one too, filling in the centre with yellow until the paper is so wet there are fuzzy paper bits floating in the paint. You work hard to cover the paper with colour. Your wrist wobbles. Green grass. A black house with square windows and pink curtains. You have painted in a second sun, which the teacher points out is incorrect. You let the extra sun dry and cover it with a big white cloud.

After recess, you stand with the others at the back of the classroom and hang your coat on a hook. You stamp your feet to warm them. The desks have been moved back into rows, and the paintings, the white paper curled and bumpy, have been stapled to bulletin boards that go as high as the ceiling and line the inside walls of the room. You look for your painting. You try to remember exactly how the paint went, on which side you painted the white cloud. You scan the dry papers with the beginning of panic, staring at thirty identical trees and houses and lawns and yellow suns.

FOUR

You walk around the carnival spending the money you saved over several weeks of babysitting. The asphalt looks different, grimier, with cotton-candy cones strewn about and fat electrical wires snaking from booth to machine. You tend to want to look under things: a glimpse of greasy gears here, an unshaven man in a

EIGHT SCENES: SOME TANGLED, SOME PLAIN

ripped T-shirt behind the dingy glass there. You aren't the kind of girls to whom such a place is magical: it is Saturday afternoon, and you mean to spend it intensely.

You have skipped Greek in order to come because Betsy was on the point of tears about it on the phone. *You can catch up,* Betsy said, and now she stands cheerfully biting into two waffles with ice cream dripping out of them, surveying the machines that can spin you about, deciding which one you should try next. The body suspended in air, the constant knowledge that the machinery could seize and throw you back onto the cement or into one of the temporary metal fences that ring every ride. Betsy won't go up alone; but once there, she thinks nothing of almost tipping the seat by swinging back and forth, or sticking her arms straight up into the air when the small paper sign in front instructs riders to hold tightly onto the bar.

You throw darts at balloons for a while, confer about the lopsided weights in them, and finally win a stuffed bear which you promptly hand to a passing woman with a pram and a three-year-old in tow. Betsy eats chips from a greasy paper bag, and cotton candy, from which you freely take large bites. You hand in tickets for the haunted house—which scares you when the cart seems to jerk sideways—for the lagoon, and for the snaky jet. The rocket looks tame enough: a machine that spins on a level platform; but it goes very quickly, and when you get off, Betsy looks green. Betsy puts her hand on your arm, and you lead her around to the back of one of the false fronts. Betsy vomits again and again, with one hand holding onto a metal strut and one hand holding back her hair. She leans over away from your shoes and coughs.

If you were a boy, you say, looking past Betsy at the people grouped around the ring toss with the fuzzy snakes hanging down and the red awning that keeps the sun off, *if you were a boy I'd want to go out with you and we could get married. It's too bad.*

F I V E

At quarter to seven you get out of bed, spend a moment in the bathroom splashing water on your sticky eyes, then head into the kitchen to start the water boiling for eggs.

You call your mother at two minutes past, just enough time for her to slip on her robe, wash, and be at the table when the toast is coming up, brown and golden.

Your mother reaches her hand out for the glass of orange juice, and sets it down again. *It's too cold*, she says, *put it back in the hot water.*

EIGHT SCENES: SOME TANGLED, SOME PLAIN

The toast, the egg, are slid in front of your mother. *This toast isn't buttered,* your mother says, *take it back and butter it to the edges as I've told you. Hurry up, it's getting cold.*

Your mother cracks the top of the egg expertly as it sits in the stainless-steel eggcup, one click of the spoon into the brown shell. *You'll have to make me another one,* your mother says, *this is overcooked.*

You move the eggcup onto your own plate and let the egg sit there, its yolk showing through the creamy white. Steam drifts up as you put the water on again to boil. You take your mother's cold toast, too.

No morning sun or birds in December, just the sound of shovelling. Cars slide through the slush outside, hot water runs from the tap into a bowl underneath the juice glass in the sink, and your mother's long nails are tapping at the teacup by her plate.

SIX

Crumpled nearly by the water and why? There is Andrea putting lunch out on a flat dry rock. The water twists in front of you like a live thing on a rope. You aren't hungry, is that it? The hour and a half deciding what to have, the later time stopping for ice and freshly squeezed juice, the endless road to get here through the suburbs of some town that shouldn't have any, the sky.

A little skill of forgetting that you do not possess. Your black car parked by itself behind the wooden barrier, shining and shining like a bottle of beer. Your mother used to bring you here when she wanted to paint, her slim brown legs sticking out of cuffed white shorts, her tattered running shoes, the broken plate she preferred as a palette in her left hand, six or seven Polaroid shots of the scene she was painting, never this one, photos of the way that other scene had looked the day before and the days before that, clipped with clothes-pins to the top of her aluminum easel.

Too much blue, you wanted to say to her then, as you sat on the sand throwing one rock into the lake for each member of your family, and you want to say it again as you turn to face your friend and find her eating.

SEVEN

You are standing on a long green slope. To your left, there are willows, ancient and trailing their branches on the ground. The air is still, and none of the willows are moving. In front of you there is a large rectangle of off-white canvas neatly covered with a thick coat of gesso. Large pieces of old china covered with paint serve as

EIGHT SCENES: SOME TANGLED, SOME PLAIN

palettes. They sit where the slats of the easel meet. Brush handles stick out of a juice tin set into a hole in the wood. You squint at the canvas and slash red paint across its white surface. The slash has crimson drips leading away from it; slops of red curl beneath the drips. You stare at the sun and as it turns your eyesight crimson you shrug. To your right, above the treetops, there is a billboard. Scores of small black birds are ranged across the billboard's upper edge, between the light standards. The birds flitter from their perch until the sky there is so full of birds that the blue seems fuzzy with feathers. You cover the canvas with paint. Your wrist wobbles: green and black and pink. You let the surface become tacky before you dip your brush into the white.

Later you stand at the back of a room by yourself and hang your jacket on a hanger. The table, desk, and chairs have been moved against the walls, and the canvases, ripped from the stretchers, are strewn on the floor at the other end of the room. You look at the painting done beside the birds rising from the billboard, you try to remember the weight of white paint on the end of a brush. Your hands become insubstantial and the light beaming through the windows is the colour of naked angels, the colour of everything you never understand.

EIGHT

You have never lived in this area and you have never been in this hospital before. It is a low, rectangular building set into the side of a hill. You release your seatbelt and step into the heat, stretching your legs after the long drive down through Tobermory and the Bruce Peninsula. You ask at the desk and are directed up the stairs, where you go, looking down through the holes between the steps, your right hand lightly touching the iron railing. A fire door and two right turns.

She is lying in a white clean bed with chrome rails shining at the sides. The back of her head is on the pillow, her white hair very thin now, scalp showing through. Her lips are grey and chapped. You carefully remove the bits of Kleenex by her cheek, announcing yourself to her softly. The room is unbearably hot, even with the curtains down, and you wonder why there are no fans, no flowers, why the unidentifiable red juice on the nightstand is in a foam cup. She has had a stroke in the past day, and one eye droops while the other shines at you.

At this point, there is no entertainment in trying to undo the past for either of you. There is only the possibility of comfort.

Are you thirsty? you ask, taking up the spoon and

EIGHT SCENES: SOME TANGLED, SOME PLAIN

cup, and she nods and opens her mouth a little. It's so hot. *I'll put the bed up a bit first, if you like,* you tell her, and go to the crank at the bottom of the bed, turning the handle slowly, not enough to leave her sitting up.

She is paralysed on the left side. Her bad hand lies still and dry on her chest. You fill the spoon with juice and pour the liquid slowly, feeling through the steel how much she has taken. She swallows and swallows, her tongue keeping the liquid away from the parts of her mouth and throat where she can't feel, where it might choke her.

You have done this before, you suppose, only it was you propped in the chair, you with the sweet happiness of comfort in your eyes, you whose little blue chambray suit was kept clean by a cloth tucked under your chin while you took food from a spoon.

Minutes go by. You see a little juice go down, you give water every few sips to clean the palate, you hold her good hand, tell her that you love her.

You both hear someone coming at the same time. The sounds of voices drift from the hallway mixed with the rumble of a drug cart. You keep on with the juice, knowing that you will soon have to go. Your aunt is here, your cousins, and their sad and pleasant noise that you don't want to hear, although you nod and say hello.

Your aunt takes the cup from you, the spoon, the seat beside the bed. You lean down and hear her whisper before you stand away. You watch your aunt pour a full spoonful flat into the middle of her parched grey mouth, watch her cough and push the spoon away with her good hand.

No one has brought a fan. There is hot still air against your face and hers. You say something you can't remember to your aunt, knowing she has been at the bedside all along, while you were not. Nothing moves as the drug cart slides by outside the door, and you expect, remembering the touch of her warm good hand, you expect to be shuddering, but you are not, because underneath it is knotted and knotted to itself, to the heat, to the day.

HELL & OTHER NOVELS

◆ A sandwich of dry brown bread and orange cheese, partly wrapped in plastic, is lying where the road meets the curb. I wonder how the things I saw abandoned on the road today—one beige loafer, a green scarf, and this sandwich—fell to the asphalt without anyone noticing. I stop to watch as three sparrows tug on the plastic wrap with darting beaks and peck at the exposed crust before they strut and flitter away into a hedge across the street. Starlings with reddish-brown feet glide down from the hydro wires and replace the sparrows, squawking.

It is the sixth of July, 1990, nearly eight weeks since my son Alexander disappeared. Forty-nine days ago I answered the telephone in the front hall and, with the cold black receiver in my hand, listened to a young man, a Vancouver friend of Alexander's, explain that Alexander had missed several days of work. The friend had become worried and started a search. He was sorry to tell me that Alexander could not be found. The young man was kind enough, but he was a busy sort of person with an eager voice. He thought I would like to know that the police had discovered my son's car in its usual spot, that they had checked his seventh-floor apartment, and that there were posters of Alexander's face stapled to telephone poles and piled on counters at the Robson Street restaurants where Alexander used to spend his evenings.

I am walking with the sun in my face along a curving grey road that separates one field of weeds from another, avoiding the facts and myself. Heat soaks through my green dress and the smell of tar drifts from farther up the street where workmen are putting a roof on a new house. Tar and hot smoke sting my eyes; a white car passes, raising dust.

For weeks I held my breath. I read and re-read *Utopia*. I read biographies of Thomas More. I wandered from one room to another in my house, touching things that had not been transformed: the peach and yellow pitcher full of milk inside the fridge; the antique shelf with its leaded glass doors; china and books and the curtains at every window. If I wailed and cried, if hot tears stained my cheeks, if I smashed porcelain figures on the floor and cut my hands cleaning up, I do not recall.

A book about Alexander's life could be a novel called *Hell*, I think. I have no evidence for this, but it doesn't matter. This friend of my son's on the telephone told me there were posters up. He said that he could see one of the posters from where he was standing in his apartment, speaking to me—it was on a pole outside his window— and that the likeness of Alexander was very good. He said, *There is nothing to be done. Our hands are tied.*

Today, July sixth, is the four hundred and fifty-fifth anniversary of the beheading of Saint Thomas More. Just after dawn on that morning, a fat guard, dressed in wool and reeking of sweat, climbed through the dark Tower of London to More's prison cell, accompanied by a messenger from Henry the Eighth. The guard lit a candle from a torch in a sconce, set it on the only table in the cell, and left More and the younger man alone. Removing his hat, the messenger bowed. He wanted to avoid More's eyes. The messenger told More two things. The first was that More was to be executed before nine o'clock that morning; the second, that if More addressed the crowd from the platform where he was to be beheaded, he was ordered by the King to be brief. The young man and More stood silent in the cell: one man containing his freedom to walk past the guard and away to breakfast with his wife; one containing his heart, blackening against the idea of the axe. Each of them knew that if More made a speech from the platform, the King's minions would twist More's hands behind his back and pull a cloth bag over his head. Such a struggle would destroy More's state of grace. The messenger knelt and asked More to bless him, which More did, muttering a prayer and kindly brushing his hand over the back of the younger man's head. As the messenger followed the guard back along the hallway to the stone stairs of the Tower, he was shaken by the words More had asked him to take to his family. Descending in the heaving orange firelight of the guard's torch, he still felt the brush of More's hand against his hair.

You have to have parameters and limits, but here I am all over the place, back in 1535 with a saint whose head was struck cruelly from his body with an axe, and walking down a suburban street in Stratford, Ontario, on July 6, 1990. I am considering the crucible in my son Alexander's life, that moment of watershed and choice. In the life of a saint, this decision is pragmatic—martyrdom becomes the only bearable option.

In order to avoid answering the door and the telephone at home, I am walking along John Street. The beautiful old trees have been cut down to make way for houses that look pre-fabricated, but are in fact modern, custom-built, brick. Our idea of what is tangible has become a little less solid.

In each of these John Street houses I can imagine the broadloom. Carpenters don't lay in hardwood any more; the floors are chipboard nailed to the joists and covered with rug that is the grey colour of old wet stone. An inoffensive muted colour that *won't show the dirt*.

Alexander's friend went to a great deal of trouble to let me know that he would be arriving in Stratford today with the keys to my son's apartment. His letter was formally typed on good linen paper. He gave me to understand that I am expected to admit myself to Alexander's rooms, discard his shabby toothbrush and his half-used soap, remove his sweaters and his kettle, take down his drawings from the walls, and to pack his things away inside the ordinary shapes of boxes.

It's hot out, but a mild summer wind doesn't help the appearance of this neighbourhood. Sod has recently been laid and is brown in artificial-looking lines where the roots didn't take or the water didn't reach. There's some green, but it's patchy. The earth, where it shows, is the dun clay colour of the bricks. There's sky, a high sky here, like in the prairies; Stratford, built on a sort of plateau, is the highest city in Ontario. Along the street I can see vacant land where farms used to be, and I can smell manure that is spread on fields farther south.

There are stickers on the new windows, because no one has had time to remove them, and curtain rods made of brass are stacked beside the sills. You can stand on the clay soil, which will need years of supplementing with mulch and peat to sustain growth, and look through the front window of any of these houses into a bare beige room. There, you will see a woman. She stands in the centre of the floor. There are no flowered chesterfields, no brass hat stands, no Wedgwood on the plate rail, no Alex Colville prints on the walls. The woman is barefoot, her shoes forgotten at the door.

The woman is standing with her eyes on nothing in particular, making a decision. She could be a 'mother,' or an 'ex-stripper' wearing a black straw hat with a little mesh veil. I could imagine her giving birth alone, or eating corn relish and pastrami from a hand-painted plate, or dancing with a demon who seems like an ordinary man with a scratchy face and dull desperate hands.

Frankly, I just don't want to have her bothered while she is concentrating. As long as I am wondering about fate, I figure I might as well imagine some company.

Walking here, there is a choice of surfaces: fresh black asphalt, steaming in the heat and smelling faintly of fire and brimstone; and, above the curb, stony land overgrown with the less attractive northern grasses, goldenrod, and Queen Anne's lace.

Thomas More was eventually beheaded for his failure to take an oath approving Henry's marriage to the six-fingered Anne Boleyn. Before it came to this extreme, however, the King's chief conspirators, Richard Rich and Thomas Cromwell, tried to make a case for More's execution based on his visit to an infamous madwoman, Mary Sloan. Mary prophesied in tongues and was suspected of heresy. Some nuns north of London permitted Mary to live in peace on their convent grounds. More, a lay judge in some church matters, did take a hand in burning heretics at the stake, but he did nothing to persecute Mary Sloan. In England at the time, it was heretical to read from a bible written in English, in particular from translations that spoke highly of poverty and simplicity in the clergy. Simple possession of the English bible often resulted in the transgressor being burned or boiled in a pot of oil in a village square. If the heretic was drawn and quartered, the severed head was later stuck on top of a pole where birds could eat the eyes. Those wishing to become martyrs courted disaster with public proclamations of their new religion, while the faithful stood about the green and, transfixed, watched the spectacle—the screams of the heretic whose hair blazed up like dry straw, or the cutting into the abdominal skin of the living heretic with a long curved blade, and the drawing out of bloody entrails by the gloved hands of church employees.

Henry the Eighth suffered from syphilis. In rage he lifted his purple sleeves like axes at his barren wife; her handmaids ran from his silken step. Thomas More wrote books of his own, but he also wrote a book under Henry's name, a pious book for priests to read. It was because of this book that the Pope conferred on Henry the title: Defender of the Faith.

A heretic's death was public and highly symbolic. Beheading was for silence. Burning was for purification; boiling in oil or drawing and quartering for humiliation. These latter methods of execution allowed the victim to recant, and official witnesses often reported that they heard the words of soul-saving conversion in the screams of the heretics before they died.

It is nice to walk along these streets. I have come to the old houses, some with turrets at the corners, the red brick hardened to a rich ochre, ancient leaded glass panes in the windows gleaming in slightly wavy squares, beautiful gardens and clipped obedient grass. And shade, at last. It is peaceful here with the sound of dogs barking and children playing tag, the tapping of old Mrs. Barton's cane, her milky smiling eyes turned toward me, her lovely soft white hair shining in the sunlight.

Is there an odd relationship between windows and television? Between me and peepers standing on the clay at night? Television writers have come up with brilliant ideas for situation comedies: a beautiful woman who is a witch (she can make people disappear, for instance, or possibly cure cancer) is married to a 'mortal' and lives in the suburbs, where she spends her time doing silly things to her neighbours and to her husband's boss; the husband is always making her put away her alien, unfair magic.

I am thinking about these magic television women because I am thinking about a woman standing stock still in a living room on John Street, although by now (I do walk quickly) I am downtown. Not much of a story, really, is this? I know I am avoiding something. This is all simply content, and the content of television is like the reasons the King gives for the things he does.

Here I am, then, walking downtown. Trying to avoid the messenger from Vancouver, but it's so quiet suddenly that it seems possible there is no one else here. Perhaps I am in the middle of an outbreak of plague. Or am I actually considering suicide, examining the labels of a multiplicity of poisons in the hardware store? Maybe I'm just walking because I had a fight with my husband, or because the sky is so high and blue today in the middle of summer.

Instead of shorts and T-shirts gracing the pedestrians around me, I can imagine the complicated dress of sixteenth-century England: laced and ruffled and split sleeves, the dark blues and maroons of the well-made cotton and wool garments worn by a man in More's position, the gold-embroidered robes of the King.

I'm in a bit of despair about my country. Will we really embrace the U.S., a nation whose public conscience encourages television shows in which abnormally small

Black children are adopted by rich white people, in which rich white people are shown to love small helpless funny powerless Black people? And is this culture so very different in any case, I wonder, as my fingers trail over the spines of paperbacks in a wooden case on the sidewalk.

I've been forgetting things lately, so I was going to sit in a dark room, and drift back, and tell you a story about the puritan heretic Mary Sloan, who once wore lovely green dresses, and who met her fiancé for readings out of the first English translation of the bible in a forest near Epping. I was going to tell you how her fiancé, Frederick Utwhich, was caught proselytizing for the new protestant religion in a tavern at Leeds, and how, on the cool October day he was executed, Mary stood at the back of the crowd with her hands over her mouth and watched in horror as he was drawn and quartered, and how she became mad at the sight of his poor face matted with blood and stuck on a pole. Mary's story would have made a nice short tragic novel, I think.

Alexander's disappearance has taken on a density and opacity which I find surprising and disappointing. It is a *fact* around which peripheral gestures of the imagination form and dissolve. (Alexander has forgotten who he *was* and has thrown himself into the ocean. He emerges from the street-level doors of Gary's Upstairs and suddenly feels his wrists gripped and twisted behind him, a cloth hood pulled over his head.) A fact, like Sarah's father disappearing, and Sarah and her mother reading about his murder in the newspaper seven years later. Facts that require resolution when there isn't any.

I am in a restaurant now, a Chinese-Canadian restaurant that serves greasy chop suey and soggy french fries. Gold-framed peacocks with real feathers in bilious versions of blue and green adorn the walls. Padded black and red chairs of curved lacquered wood are snug against the tables. The cream is an edible oil product, and the coffee is tasty but weak.

A few blocks from here, a gentleman named Frederick Utwhich is sitting in his living room on Mornington Street, just past the river which splits Stratford in two. He has my notebook, which I probably left outside the bookstore when I was considering the purchase of a pristine copy of Madeleine Gagnon's *Lair*. I know I did leave my other package there, because I went back down the street looking for it and found it on top of the paperbacks in the wooden case. My name is in the notebook that I lost, and my phone number, but I am not at home.

It is possible that I am sixty-five years old, or fifty-three, or forty, that my other children were stillborn or are grown and living in other Canadian cities, that my husband is dead or has left me or is wondering where I am, that I was not arguing with him at all, but shouting at my cat to get out of the ivy pot before I left the house.

Frederick Utwhich has the television on, though it is only four in the afternoon. He picks up my notebook, which is full of ideas and small scenes from half-written novels, and he puts it down again. He finds it hard to decipher the handwriting, and the first entry puts him off:

you had planned the kidnapping for weeks, but debbie, who had also just turned fourteen, didn't believe you were serious until she saw the gun in your hand. the idea was to capture a man, preferably one in a suit, because they seemed easier, and to keep him for a while in the deserted house you'd found.

there was a chair in that house, and rope. you had already covered the windows with newspaper and tape, and repaired them daily if wind or rain got through where the glass was broken. the idea was to make him strip, tie him up, examine him carefully, then make him answer questions about sex. an hour would do it, you thought, an hour or so, then untie him and send him off again.

you spent a lot of time standing still in the front room of that house beside the road, trying to pick which one, which man in which car.

The temptation is to tell a nice story. About Mary Sloan, for instance, and her relationship with her uncle, who was a bad priest with a good heart, and his common-law wife. The three of them shared the large and cold stone parish house by Glen Epping.

Did I remember to tell you that I bought poison at the hardware store? Did I tell you that the only extant drawing of Frederick Utwhich shows his dark eyes and English pallor, his wavy fine black hair, which no amount of pushing back could keep from curling over his forehead? Did I explain that his face could have been Alexander's face? I see one thing turning into another thing before my eyes, and once the transformation has been effected (from Chancellor of London to martyr, for instance) there is a terrible danger of becoming confused.

The song of the same bird wakes Frederick Utwhich at five every morning. He has never seen it, but as he lies awake and listens, he imagines the shape of the bird. He wants to hold it tenderly in his hands, to touch its cold feathers and sharp black beak.

Frederick has cancer, which is only a disease because it doesn't know when to stop. If cancer only took what it needed, Frederick thinks, he could go on living and the cancer could, too.

I am thinking about Thomas More because something he imagined allowed him to bare the back of his neck calmly for the executioner's axe. Frederick Utwhich reads:

the first Canadian nobel prize-winner for literature, Vincente Sangrelli, lies dying, working on a long poem which is transcribed daily by his faithful wife and his son. the poetry is gibberish, and his wife rewrites most of it.

Frederick recognizes this as pure melodrama, and puts my notebook down on his TV tray, which displays a very nice painting of Canada geese flying over marshy land in formation. His television is a perpetual flame in the corner of his living room.

I was examining a copy of *Polytechnique, 6 décembre*, an anthology of feminist writing about the day a man who could not get a place in the best engineering school in Montreal took a gun and shot fourteen women there to death, most of them students, and I came across this quote from Alain Robbe-Grillet: 'To be sure, in the world of male fantasy, woman's body serves as the ideal site for the crime.'

After that I couldn't read forward in the book any more. The woman is still standing in the middle of the living room, in the middle of the stone-coloured floor. I should think Robbe-Grillet would be quite frightened if she began to move toward him, brushing him at first with her hand to let him know that she was there.

Frederick hates television, even though he believes that it allows him to go out into places he would never otherwise see. Television sucks him out of his own life and makes him a part of an invisible crowd rioting in private, safe and distant from what incites it. Television is like a very bad story no one wrote, reading itself to him from a corner of the room, a story that never ends and yet is not a comedy, a story written by a committee in a hurry to get it over with and go out and get drunk, a story that exhausts him with its unrelated characters, its seven thousand simultaneous situations.

Four young people in bathing-suits with exaggerated smiles are beckoning to Frederick. They are singing wildly about chewing gum. Frederick considers the things people have sung songs about through recorded history: gods and love, death and loss and favourite countrysides. Frederick is very fond of Stompin' Tom Connors, and particularly fond of the song 'Sudbury Saturday Night,' which he recalls going: *The girls are out to bingo and the boys are gettin' stinko / we think no more of Inco on a Sudbury Saturday night.* Frederick thinks television is shrinking his concept of eternity. He remembers standing in line at the bank, the greasy sausage smell of the man behind him, breathing impersonal, pre-used air. Television and the registered trademark for Coca-Cola Limited are going to outlive him. What more of eternity can he possibly imagine? The 'boys in the Gulf,' waiting for war, smile at the camera for Frederick in his living room.

I am still in the restaurant. A young African-Canadian man with close-cropped hair and a young Chinese-Canadian woman, both of whom work here, are talking at the next table. Part of me is listening to them: she plays old-fashioned English instruments, she says, the zither, the lute, a recorder made of wood. He is working his way through the dental course at the local university. Watching their dark heads, his elegant and bent toward their conversation, hers smooth and almost blue against the haze rising from the French cigarettes they are both smoking, and the light through the front window, the empty hangers on the metal coat rack, I misplace my pen. Part of me is thinking about the heretic, Mary Sloan, soaking up soup made of barley and beef bones with a hank of bread, dreaming of Epping Forest and Frederick with his beautiful eyes waiting for her there.

Television does not stop to let Frederick think. He sits drinking. After a while he begins to sob without knowing why. Nothing moves outside the window. It is becoming dark. The television grinds on with or without his attention. Like an accessory, Frederick watches. His fingers grip a cold glass of Scotch as a man in a dark overcoat is shot several times. The wounded man falls backwards, over the low railing, off the building, and the camera follows his body down, past the windows, to the sickening crunch of bones and skull against cement. The bad are killed and killed again, but they keep coming. Frederick is afraid to move or to turn on the light on the table beside him. He hears the disembodied laughter of the invisible crowd he is among, hushed and waiting as David Cronenberg's Fly rips into another victim's abdominal skin with a long curved claw.

Mary Sloan sneaks out of the convent to meet the remaining members of the sect. The forest is dark. There are wild boars, poachers, highwaymen. She risks being burned, but this is a lowly and pedestrian matter to Mary. She moves aside the ivy so as not to damage it as she climbs over the wall. She does not feel the clammy cold stone as she climbs, or the thorns cutting into her thighs. The nuns will not miss her; she spends most of her time in the shadows, crouching on damp, fetid earth. Heavy lower leaves of the hawthorn brush against her hair as she emerges into the open woods. What if the nuns (the kind nuns who serve her bread and cheese and apples on a wooden board, who give her clean grey underclothes and dresses to wear) won't let her back in? She imagines them in their separate cells, those bare stone rooms with tiny windows high in the walls, hard wooden beds with wooden crosses above them, thin metal bands on the third fingers of their left hands. She has forgotten every look of Frederick's except his face melting on the pole. Mary hurries through the forest, dry leaves underfoot, and prays that she will not be discovered, that she has not forgotten to replace the flat leaves of the ivy. She has left her shoes behind and it is getting cold, but this cannot be helped. That night, before the fire, the huddled heretics are amazed to hear how much of the Book of Mark she has memorized in English.

I have been leafing through a copy of *Life* magazine, wondering what happened to my pen (and here it is, under a serviette). Elvis Presley, an article says, killed himself with drugs. Did he choke on his own vomit on the bathroom floor? Who prescribed him which barbiturates? How many times did he have to be outfitted with new costumes because of his ballooning weight? Beside the picture of the bathroom where Elvis died there is a glossy advertisement for automobiles. A family outside a church is there to sell slacks. And then lovely grainy photographs of a crack slum in Philadelphia. Photomontage, pages of beautiful Black children in torn white T-shirts proffering guns or standing beside broken windows. A pimp grips the shoulder of a tired, magical-looking woman. A young boy gazes in through the window of an old Chevrolet, at blood smeared on the white interior, at a man with a bullethole through his temple lying sprawled across the front seat; the picture, in black and white, taken with such attention to composition.

In sixteenth-century England, death by hanging was reserved for thieves. An honest man could sit by the roadside where fences around the new enclosures (sheep grazing for the lucrative wool trade) kept him off the land that used to be his farm, and watch his family starve, or he could steal a sheep and kill it and feed his children. Mary Sloan's uncle attended the hangings of his parishioners with bent head, unmoving, his lips tormented by the inadequate Latin of the services he spoke. Although heads were occasionally torn from necks in their plunge from the gallows, it was not important to the King to separate the heads of thieves from their bodies. There was humiliation enough in the involuntary display of bodily functions. A hung corpse usually twisted in the wind for days, falling only when the neck had rotted through.

An element of humiliation, certainly. Frederick's television screen has gone fuzzy. Wavy lines extend from one side to the other, accompanied by a noise like that of an electric saw or a vacuum cleaner. With his knees denting the deep plush carpeting of his living-room floor, he twists the knobs, turns the serrated wheels recessed under the screen.

What we didn't learn about Thomas More's meeting

with the heretic Mary Sloan under the hanging vines before, we see played out in Frederick's living room now. Frederick Utwhich stood on the platform in the green and sensed that Mary was somewhere in the crowd. The implements lay beside him on the grey dusty wood: the tub and the chains, the knives (for he was not the only martyr on that hot October day) and the silent excited men who were about to torture him. With his head slightly bowed, Frederick scanned the faces in the whispering crowd; he smelled sweat, sausage, felt his own armpits trickling. Frederick believed in ultimate redemption. He prayed for the salvation of those who were preparing to murder him, but he was not a fool. He did not imagine that ordinary strength could sustain his dignity during the ordeal he was about to undergo. Frederick's hands were locked together before him, his feet firmly placed in their brown boots on the platform. When he saw the flash of Mary's white collar in the crowd, toward the back beside a brick wall festooned with coloured streamers, her eyes closed and her hands folded in supplication, he fell to his knees and began to intone the Lord's Prayer aloud in English so that all before him could understand. They gasped, as he wanted them to, as if an angel had descended among them. And when it began to happen, when he was gripped from behind by the shoulders and his wrists were bound cruelly with rope, a cloth hood pulled over his head, he had already stopped feeling. That is the story Mary told Thomas More, but she was not in London on the day of Frederick's passion. To prevent her, her uncle had her tied to a rocking chair. Mary Sloan was mad, and only imagined she had been a witness to Frederick's death, but her story made up Thomas More's mind and gave him the strength to suffer his own martyrdom.

Frederick makes a decision; he leaves the house. It is a pleasant July evening, and twenty bluebirds rise up out of the hedge as he closes his wooden front gate. White clouds drift across the black sky as Frederick makes his way toward the river where the swans sail through the summer. He wants to see them open their wings, that's all.

I'm not crazy, I don't think. I simply believe that, considering the circumstances of my failure, a test is in order. Choice between one thing and another has been at the back of my mind all day. As the weeks have gone by I have become less and less obsessed with the indelible facts (the keys to Alexander's apartment in a linen envelope lying beneath the mail slot on my hallway floor; Alexander's face, his hair in his eyes, staring out from a hundred telephone poles) and I accept how hard it is to understand the way one thing can seem to be transformed into something simpler, less painful, less deceptive.

In front of me there are two cups. One contains tea and the strychnine I bought this afternoon at the hardware store, and the other cup contains only sweet hot tea with milk. I tell myself to remember which is which as I turn them about on the table, as I steel my tongue not to reject bitterness if that is what it finds, as I touch the hard curved porcelain of the handles: one cup and the other cup. It is essential to remember what is important, I think, as I reach out my hand in the dark.

Mary Sloan was burned at the stake as a witch on December 7, 1537, after she had taught herself to read English well enough to begin attempting to convert the nuns to puritanism. Because of her protestant leanings, her martyrdom was never rewarded with beatification.

Frederick Utwhich sits by the river with his face in his hands, for he has seen no swans. Something brushes across the back of his head and he immediately looks up and across at the lighted houses reflected in the river. At this moment he believes that death is brushing against him. He believes that death is becoming familiar with the shape of him. But Frederick is wrong. He has been the subject of a miracle, and when next he goes for treatment it will be discovered that his cancer is gone. This happens, you know, though very rarely; that something haunting and deadly simply disappears, and leaves you perfect and cured.

A note on the text: In 'Hell & Other Novels,' I have taken some minor liberties with history. The actual heretic visionaries whose acquaintance endangered Thomas More were Elizabeth Barton, also known as the Nun of Kent, whom he met at a monastery, and Anne Wentworth—not Mary Sloan. Elizabeth Barton's lover was named Edward Bocking.

In April, 1534, at Tyburn, England, Barton was hanged, cut down while still living and drawn and quartered. Bocking later met a similar fate.

Guest Editor for the Press: Gail Scott
Editor for the Press: Susan Swan
Design: Shari Spier / Reactor
Cover Illustration: Jamie Bennett
Printed in Canada

COACH HOUSE PRESS
401 (rear) Huron Street
Toronto, Canada
M5S 2G5